Marx Joyce
Abbott Hardy Montaigne Machiavelli Chesterton Cooper Emerson Austen
Defoe Melville Haggard Hugo
Christie Carroll Eliot Grimm
Stoker Molière
Wilde Maupassant Byron
Engels Schiller
Garnett Einstein Fitzgerald Smith
Goethe Hawthorne Kafka
Cotton Dostoyevsky Hall
Baum Kipling Doyle Willis
Leslie Dumas Henry Nietzsche
Flaubert Turgenev Balzac
Stockton Vatsyayana Crane
Burroughs Whitman
Verne
Curtis Tocqueville Gogol Vinci
Homer Widger Tolstoy Busch
Darwin Thoreau
Potter Freud Twain Plato Scott
Zola Lawrence
Kant Jowett Stevenson Dickens
Andersen Burton Hesse Harte
London Descartes Cervantes
Poe Aristotle Wells Voltaire
Hale James Hastings
Bunner Shakespeare Cooke
Richter Chambers Irving
Doré Swift Dante Chekhov da Shaw Wodehouse Benedict Alcott
Pushkin
Newton

tredition®

tredition was established in 2006 by Sandra Latusseck and Soenke Schulz. Based in Hamburg, Germany, tredition offers publishing solutions to authors and publishing houses, combined with worldwide distribution of printed and digital book content. tredition is uniquely positioned to enable authors and publishing houses to create books on their own terms and without conventional manufacturing risks.

For more information please visit: www.tredition.com

TREDITION CLASSICS

This book is part of the TREDITION CLASSICS series. The creators of this series are united by passion for literature and driven by the intention of making all public domain books available in printed format again - worldwide. Most TREDITION CLASSICS titles have been out of print and off the bookstore shelves for decades. At tredition we believe that a great book never goes out of style and that its value is eternal. Several mostly non-profit literature projects provide content to tredition. To support their good work, tredition donates a portion of the proceeds from each sold copy. As a reader of a TREDITION CLASSICS book, you support our mission to save many of the amazing works of world literature from oblivion. See all available books at www.tredition.com.

Project Gutenberg

The content for this book has been graciously provided by Project Gutenberg. Project Gutenberg is a non-profit organization founded by Michael Hart in 1971 at the University of Illinois. The mission of Project Gutenberg is simple: To encourage the creation and distribution of eBooks. Project Gutenberg is the first and largest collection of public domain eBooks.

The Fatal Jealousie (1673)

Henry Nevil Payne

Imprint

This book is part of TREDITION CLASSICS

Author: Henry Nevil Payne
Cover design: Buchgut, Berlin – Germany

Publisher: tredition GmbH, Hamburg - Germany
ISBN: 978-3-8424-8276-0

www.tredition.com
www.tredition.de

CONTENTS

INTRODUCTION

None of Henry Nevil Payne's plays, *The Fatal Jealousie* (1673), *The Morning Ramble* (1673), *The Siege of Constantinople* (1675), bears his name on the title-page. Plenty of external evidence exists, however, to prove his claim to them. John Downes, in *Roscius Anglicanus* (1708), has this to say: "*Loves Jealousy* [i.e. *The Fatal Jealousy*], and *The Morning Ramble*. Written by Mr. *Nevil Pain*. Both were very well *Acted*, but after their first run, were laid aside, to make Room for others; the Company having then plenty of new Poets" (ed. Montague Summers, London, n.d., pp. 33-34). "After the Tempest, came the Siege of *Constantinople*, Wrote by Mr. *Nevill Pain*" (*ibid.*, p. 35). Langbaine's *An Account of the English Dramatick Poets* (1691) gives no author for *The Siege of Constantinople*, but says of *The Fatal Jealousy* that it is "ascribed by some to Mr. Pane" (p. 531) and of *The Morning Ramble* that this "Play is said to be written by One Mr. *Pane*, and may be accounted a good Comedy" (p. 541).

We do not have to depend on the early historians of the English drama for certain knowledge that Payne was for a time a dramatist. Though his brief excursion into the theater must later have seemed to him a minor episode in his life, Payne's enemies were aware of the fact that he was a playwright and have written their knowledge into the record of his treasonable activities. For example, the author of a burlesque life of Payne, which contains, so far as I know, the only connected account of his activities, makes this useful remark: "Then [after his return from Ireland in 1672] he composes a Tragedy of a certain Emperour of Constantinople, whom he never knew; but in whose person he vilifies a certain Prince [Charles II], whom he very well knows" (*Modesty Triumphing over Impudence* ... 1680, pp. 18-19).

As an agent of the Catholic party, Payne had excellent reasons for wishing to keep his affairs well veiled. What we know of his life has had to be pieced together from information 2 found in state papers, court records, and "histories" of the branches of the damnable Popish plots.* The date of his birth is not known, nor of his death, unless Summers was correct in giving it (without supporting evidence) as 1710 (*The Works of Aphra Behn*, 1915, V, 519).

Payne's first opportunity to serve the Catholic party came, apparently, in 1670, when he went to Ireland in the employ of Sir Elisha Leighton, who was private secretary to the new lord lieutenant, Lord Berkeley. By April 1672 Berkeley's pro-Catholic rule had so alienated the city council of Dublin that he was ordered to return to England and the Earl of Essex was sent out in his place. From Essex we learn that Payne was deeply involved in the machinations of Berkeley and that he continued to stir up trouble in Ireland even after his return to England.

Back in England, possibly by mid-May, 1672, Payne must have plunged at once into work for the theater. *The Fatal Jealousy* was performed at the Duke's Theatre in Dorset Garden in August 1672 and *The Morning Ramble* was shown at the same theater three months later. Both plays were performed before the King (Allerdyce Nicoll, *A History of Restoration Drama*, 1923, p. 309). Payne's third and last play, *The Siege of Constantinople*, which reached the stage in November 1674, is of particular interest in view of his long association with the cause of James, Duke of York. Payne found his plot in the *General Historie of the Turkes* by Knolles, but he altered history to produce a work which would compliment James. It is significant that there is no prototype in Knolles for Thomazo (James), the brother of the last Christian emperor of Constantinople (Charles). At the end of the play the Turks conquer the city (*sc.*, the Dutch and London) and the Emperor is slain. Here was a warning to Englishmen of what would happen if their double-dealing "Lord Chancellor" (Shaftesbury)--the 3 villain of the piece--were to succeed in alienating the two royal brothers.

During the years 1678-1680 Payne's name dodges in and out of the thousands of words written about the Popish plot. He was pretty certainly a friend of Edward Coleman (Secretary to the Duchess of York) who was executed for treason in December, 1678. After a hearing before the Privy Council, Payne was held over for trial and imprisoned in the King's Bench. Confinement did not in the least hinder him from giving aid to the Catholic party in organizing its counter-attack. According to *Mr. Tho. Dangerfields Particular Narrative* (1679) he was one of the chief devisers of the Presbyterian Plot and, as "chief Pen-man" for the Catholics, the author of several "scandalous books" about their enemies. Payne was again before the

Privy Council in November 1679, but eventually all the principals in the Catholic plots to discredit the government were released.

After the accession of James II Payne kept more respectable company. References to him during these years say nothing about any work for the theater, but his pen was still busy--from 1685 to 1687 in the cause of religious toleration. In 1685 the Duke of Buckingham published *A Short Discourse upon the Reasonableness of Men's having a Religion or Worship of God.* A portion of this pamphlet had been written as a letter to Payne. When Buckingham's work brought on a pamphlet war, Payne (together with William Penn) rushed to his defence. The debate grew hotter when James made the first Declaration of Indulgence in April 1687. Payne was one of the chief controversialists in the war of words that followed. Another literary friend of these years, and an extravagant admirer of his devotion to the Stuarts, was Aphra Behn. She dedicated her *Fair Jilt* to Payne in 1688 in terms which suggest that he had favored her in tangible ways.

With the deposition of James, the years of Payne's greatest activity begin. The story of his life for the next twelve years is intricate and exciting, for he has now moved out of 4 the company of writers into the dark world of secret agents and prison-guards. Though he was confined in the Fleet by January 1688/89, Payne went boldly ahead with plans for what would be the first Jacobite conspiracy, the Montgomery Plot. By some means he contrived to escape to Scotland, where his plans had, of course, more fertile soil in which to grow. Once more in custody, he was moved from one prison to another, but the Privy Council was incapable of persuading the Scottish authorities to "put the rogue to it." As more and more evidence came out showing how deeply involved Payne was in the Montgomery Plot, the Scottish Privy Council finally was prevailed upon to put Payne to the torture. On Dec. 10, 1690, he bore the pain of two hours under thumb and leg screws with such fortitude that some of the Councilors were "brangled" and believed that his denials must be the words of an honest man. The Earl of Crawford, one of the witnesses to this, the last occasion in Britain in which a political prisoner was tortured, was so moved that he reported to the Earl of Melville that such manly resolution could come only from a deep religious fervor: "[Payne] did conceive he was acting a thing not only generous towards his friends and accomplices, but likewise so meritorious, that he would thereby save his soule, and be canoniz'd among the saints" (*Letters ... to George Earl of Melville,* Bannatyne Club, 1843, pp. 582-3).

For nearly eleven years more Payne was moved from one Scottish prison to another, while the Scottish Privy Council sought to turn him over to the English and the Privy Council in London endeavored to force him to trial in Scotland. The truth is that Jacobitism was so rife in high places that they whose duty it would be to prosecute him feared what might happen if he were brought to the bar.

Finally, in February 1700/01, Payne was released. He made his way to the Stuart court at St. Germain, whose incorruptible secret agent he had been for twelve years. It was fitting that the last information we have of him during his life is derived from his "Brief memorial by way of preface to some proposals for your Majesty's service," a detailed letter 5 of advice instructing the exiled king how he might yet recapture his throne (printed in *Original Papers; containing the Secret History of Great Britain,* 1775, I, 602-5). When last heard from, Payne had yet another conspiracy planned and ripened, to submit to his sovereign's approval.

Payne's *Fatal Jealousy* has intrinsic merit. If he had written more works for the theater, he might have been remembered with Southerne and possibly with Otway. But for the scholar this tragedy will be chiefly interesting for the Shakespearean influences to be found in it. Evidently Payne held Shakespeare in great reverence, and the result is that *The Fatal Jealousy* is one of the earliest examples of the return to the Shakespearean norm in tragedy after the interlude of the heroic play. Payne ridicules the love and honor theme in *The Morning Ramble* where he makes Rose say (p. 54):

Love and Honour are the two great Wheels, on which all business moves. The Tradesman cheats you upon his Honour, and like a Lord swears by that, but that he particularly loves you, you should not have it so. No Tragedy, Comedy, Farse, Demi-Farse, or Song nowadayes, but is full of Love and Honour: Your Coffee-drinking Crop-ear'd Little Banded-Secretary, that pretends not to know more of Honour than it's Name, will out of abundance of Love be still sighing and groaning for the Honour of the Nation.

The speaker of the Epilogue to *The Fatal Jealousy* pointedly reminds the audience that they have listened to a genuine tragedy and not to an heroic play. Its author has not relied on the "rules of art," but hopes he may have succeeded by some "Trick of Nature."

Most obvious of the Shakespearean influences is the jealousy theme in which Don Antonio is modelled on Othello, Caelia on Desdemona, and Jasper on Iago. My colleague, Professor E.L. Hubler, who has a vast deal of the Shakespearean text in his memory, finds twenty-two possible echoes or parallels. Of these we agree that at least fourteen are certain. The influences strike in most impressively from *Othello, Hamlet, Much Ado, Midsummer Night's Dream,* and *The Tempest.* Let me cite two or three unmistakable echoes. Jasper's 6 manner of arousing Antonio's jealousy (pp. 17-19) and even his words recall Iago's mental torturing of the Moor in *Othello,* III, 3. Throughout Gerardo's soliloquy on death, at the opening of Act III, there is continuous reference to Hamlet's "To be or not to be." The antecedent of "madness methodiz'd" (p. 35) is easily spotted, as is the parallel between Flora's dream (p. 63) which will not leave her head and the song that will not go from Desdemona's mind. So far as I can discover, the seekers for Shakespearean allusions in seventeenth-century writing have not located this rich mine.

It is to be regretted that when *The Fatal Jealousy* came to the stage the company had, as Downes says, "plenty of new poets," and so the play was laid aside after the first run. The performance must have been brilliant. The greatest of Restoration stage villains, Sandford, played Jasper. The parts of Caelia, Eugenia, and the Witch were taken by veteran actors. "Mr. Nath. Leigh" made his second appearance on the stage in this performance as Captain of the Watch. The lecherous Nurse to Caelia was played by the famous Nokes whose sobriquet of "Nurse Nokes" may have come to him with this rôle rather than from the part he took, seven years later, in Otway's *Caius Marius.*

The text of *The Fatal Jealousy* presents no special difficulties. Such slight variations as I have found among the eleven copies I have examined--chiefly dropped letters and the imperfect impression of some words--can be accounted for as accidents to be expected in the printing off of the sheets of a single edition. There seems to be no significance in the fact that the title-page in some copies shows an ornament placed between the second rule and the word *London*.

The copy of the play here reproduced is owned by the University of Michigan, and is reprinted by permission.

WILLARD THORP
Princeton University

* For this biographical sketch of Payne I have drawn on my "Henry Nevil Payne, Dramatist and Jacobite Conspirator," published in *The Parrott Presentation Volume*, Princeton, 1935, pp. 347-381.

THE

Fatal Jealousie.

A

TRAGEDY.

Acted at the Duke's Theatre.

Licensed *Novemb. 22, 1672.*

Roger L'Estrange.

LONDON,

Printed for *Thomas Dring*, at the *White Lyon*, next *Chancery-Lane* end in *Fleet-street*. 1673.

The Actors Names.

Don Antonio.	*A Jealous Lord.*	*Mr.* Smith.
Don Gerardo.	*Friend to* Antonio.	*Mr.* Medburn.
Don Francisco.	*A Young Lord.*	*Mr.* Young.
Don Sebastian.	*Friend to* Francisco.	*Mr.* Crosby.
Jasper. *A Villain.*	*Servant to* Antonio.	*Mr.* Sandford.
Pedro.	*Servant to* Antonio.	*Mr.* Burford.
Servant	*To* Gerardo.	*Mr.* Norris.
Captain of the Watch.		*Mr.* Nath. Leigh.

Souldiers.

Women.

Cælia.	*Wife to* Antonio.	*Mrs.* Shadwel.
Eugenia.	*Sister to* Cælia.	*Mrs.* Betterton.
Flora.	*Waiting Woman to* Cælia.	*Mrs.* Osborn.
Nurse	*To* Cælia.	*Mr.* Nokes.
Witch.	*Aunt to* Jasper.	*Mrs.* Norris.

Spirits.

Gipsies.

A2

PROLOGUE

By Mr. *Smith.*

TO you, great Sovereign Wits, that have such sway,
Without Controul to save, or damn a Play;
That with a pish, my Anthony, or so,
Can the best Rally'd sence at once or'e throw;
And by this pow'r, that none must question now,
Have made the most Rebellious Writers bow,
Our Author, here his low Submission brings,
Begging your pass, calls you the Stages Kings;
He sayes, nay, on a Play-Book, swears it too,
Your pox uppo'nt damn it, what's here to do?
Your nods, your winks, nay, your least signs of Wit,
Are truer Reason than e're Poet writ,
And he observes do much more sway the Pit.
For sitting there h' has seen the lesser gang
Of Callow Criticks down their heads to bang;
Lending long Ears to all that you should say,
So understand, yet never hear the Play:
Then in the Tavern swear their time they've lost,
And Curse the Poet put e'm to that cost.
And if one would their just Exceptions know,
They heard such, such, or such a one say so;
And thus in time by your dislikes they rise,
To be thought Judges, though indeed but spyes.
This is not fair your Subjects to betray
To those that strive to Rival you in sway;
That will in time by your expence of wit,
Usurp or'e us, and your successors sit.
These and some other dangers to remove,
We beg that though this Play you disapprove,
Say nothing of it here, and when you're gone,
We give that leave you'le take to cry it down;
Thus you preserve your pow'r, and we shall be

From Fopps, and Demi-Criticks Censure free.

Subdu'd by force, we Tyrants thus obey,
But Ladys, you like lawful Monarches sway,
You Rule by Love, and Pardon faults with ease,
In Subjects that do all they can to please.
By faction they condemn, you by our Peers,
And he is guilty sure such Trial fears:
And though our Author pleads not guilty now.
And to his Tryal stands, he hopes that you,
Will not too strictly his accusers hear,
For if this Play can draw from you a Tear,
He'l slight the Wits, Half-Wits, and Criticks too;
And Judge his strength by his well pleasing you.

1B

THE

Fatal Jealousie.

Act the First. Scene the First.

The Curtain drawn Discovers Don Antonio and Cælia in Morning-Gowns. Chamber and Bed.

Cæl.
MY Lord, you well may blame my conduct of that bus'ness,
Since it produc'd such dismal Accidents,
As my heart trembles but to think upon;
Yet for *Don Lewis*'s Innocence and mine,
In the contrivance of that Fatal Meeting;
I must for ever, during Life, be Champion.
And, as he with his dying breath protested,
He ne're meant wrong to you; so am I ready
To dye a Martyr to my Innocence.

Anto. Come, come, these are but wyles to Palliate things,
Can you believe me stupid, or an Ass?
To think my Wife should meet a Man i' th' Night;
Nay, more; a Man that was my seeming Friend;
Yet taken in at Window privately!
Nay, which was most, stay with him two full hours,
And in a Room made proper by a Bed,
And yet not Cuckold me; the thing's too plain,
I do not doubt the deed, which Iv'e Reveng'd
In part, by killing him: No, I am mad,
That you should think so meanly still of me,
As to hope time may alter my belief;
2 Which is by such unerring Reasons fixt:
Or else that you suspect my Truth, when I have sworn
By all things sacred; nay upon my Honour
(Which I am so Jealous of) that if you would
Relate the truth of your so close amours,
I from my memory would blot it all,

And look on you at worst, but as the Widdow
Of your dead Couzen *Lewis*.

*Cæl.*Good my Lord,
Forbear to use these killing Arguments,
Which every moment give me many Deaths,
Rather be like your self, that's Gen'rous,
And kill me once for all; torment me not
By giving no belief, either to Vows
Or Actions that have spoke my Innocence:
Reflect (my Lord) on the unwearied pains
Iv'e took to gain your pardon for his Death.
Think with what patience I've suffer'd still
Your often starts of Passion, which sometimes
Have ne're produc'd th' effects of Cruelty.
And without boast, my Lord, you well do know
My Friends were much too strong for yours at Court,
Then had I but made known your severe Carriage,
Or suffer'd your surprizal—'tis too plain;
Yoor Life had been a forfeit to the Law.
And were I but the wanton Wife you think me,
What wou'd more welcome be then that Revenge—
Here on my knees I beg again, my Lord,
You would perswade your self, that what I told you
Was cause of that close meeting, was so truly,
And no invention; and as this Day
Began our Nuptial Joys, so let it end
Our Marriage Discords; then shall I have cause
To keep it Annually a Festival;
In thanks to Heav'n for two such mighty Blessings.

Anto. Cælia, stand up, I will perswade my self.
By this —— I will as much, as e're I can,

[Kisses her.

3B2

That thou art Innocent, for if thou bee'st not,
What Woman in the World ought to be thought so?
But prethee be discreet, mannage thy Actions

With strictest Rules of Prudence, for if not,
Like to a Bow or'e-bent, I shall start back,
And break with passion on thee: wilt thou be careful?

Cæl. Oh! I am paid for all my sufferings,
This kindness does or'e-joy me, which, my Lord,
Let me for ever lose when any Act
Of mine, shall justly make a forfeit of it.

Enter Flora.

Flor. My Lord, here's *Don Gerardo* come to see you.

Anto. Admit him in.

[Exit Flora.

*Cæl.*I will retire, my Lord.

Anto. You need not, *Cælia.*

[Enter Gerardo.

Welcome, *Gerardo,* this is like a Friend,
That name should know no Ceremonious Laws,
Let them make formal Visits that maintain,
As formal Friendships; ours is try'd and true.

Gerar. This, as I take it, was your Wedding-day,
At which (your pardon, Madam, for a truth.)
I was a Jealous waiter; your great worth
Made me to fear I then had lost a Friend,
And in that room should an acquaintance find.

Cæl. But now, my Lord, you see how you mistook,
I was a Rival to his Mistresses,
But to his Friends, one to increase their number.

Ger. I find the truth so great, I wish you may
Live long and happy to possess that place;
Yet I'le confess I did not lose my fears,
Till my dear Friend was pleas'd to use my Sword,
As Second, in the Quarrel with your Kinsman,
The Unfortunate *Don Lewis;* and I protest

Such Joy I met to be employ'd by him,
That I ne're sought to know what caus'd the quarrel.

Cæl. My Lord, I beg your pardon,
I have some little bus'ness in my Closet
4 Which forces me retire.

Ger. Your Lady looks as if she were displeas'd.

Anto. That Kinsman whom I slew is never nam'd,
But if she hears it she avoids the place.

Ger. I'm troubled much to be th' occasion now.

Anto. No matter, Friend, she only knows the cause,
Why from such Friendship we grew Enemies,
And there is reason why she should be griev'd.

Ger. That sudden and so secret Quarrel
Did much amaze all *Naples*;
And I (as Actor in it) often have been prest
To tell the cause, which yet I never could.

Anto. No, Friend, nor never must:
The Gen'rous *Lewis*; so I'le call him now,
Since he so bravely dy'd, was alwayes just
During that little time he breath'd this Air;
After his mortal Wound, for he Related
A Story of it fitted us for pardon:
Yet never told that Secret, only known
On Earth, to him, to *Cælia* and my self.

Ger. I'me not inquisitive, nor never was,
There may be secrets fit for no Mans hearing.
And 'tis an Act of Friendship full as great
To tell a Friend I hide a secret from him,
As to Relate it, since they both shew Candor—

Anto. Happy *Antonio*, in a Friend so just!

Ger. Happy *Gerardo*, rather, that can say
He's sure he has a Friend, that dares employ him;
For confidence in Friends makes Friendship sure.

Anto. And dearest Friend, I'le not doubt yours so much,
To think you would not use this Life of mine,
As 'twere your own in any thing concerns you.

Ger. Ne're doubt it, Friend, I soon shall find occasion
Boldly to use the power, and to speak truth;
My coming now was chiefly to that purpose;
Though I intended to spend this day too
In Recreation with you, and to see you Bedded,
Like a new Bride and Bride-groom,
Then wishing you long: long and lasting Joys,
Retire, and wish to Copy out your Life.

Anto. Has *Don Gerardo* Service for *Antonio*,
His own *Antonio* and yet defers to name it?
Speak your Commands, that I as swift may flye
To put 'em into Action as I did
At first to meet those pleasures Lovers long for.

Ger. My fears perswade me I shall speak too soon,
Yet dress your self, and come into the Garden,
I with impatience there will wait to tell you.

Anto. Go then, you shall not long be silent.

[Ex. Gerardo.

Who waits there?

[Enter Pedro, and Exit.

Pedro, call my Wife—
My Wife, said I! *Gerardo*, didst thou know
The secret fears contain'd within this Bosome,
Thou'dst sooner pitty me, than wish my Life:
How can I think her story of the Jewels,
And other matters 'bout her Fathers Will,
Could have produc'd so scandalous a Meeting?
And yet she still avows it! Oh, Jealousie!
Where will these panting fears still hurry me?
I hourly seek to find what I wou'd give,
A thousand Worlds my heart would ne're believe;
And yet for what do I thus vex my self?

For that, which if 'twas gone, I cou'd not miss;
No, would I could, for then I'de never fear,
But when I found her Honour gone astray,
I'd send her Life to fetch mine back again.

Enter Cælia.

Cæl. What's your Command, my Lord?

Anto. Prethee, my Dear, do not retire too much,
But shew a merry freedom to our Friends,
That they may think us happy, themselves welcome.

Cæl. My Lord, I shall, and reason have to do it;
But I desire you would dispence my absence,
Only a little time, I being preparing
6 A general Confession I shall make to Morrow.

Anto. You'l be too long about it.

Cæl. No, my Lord, I take the shortest way
In writing what my thoughts can re-collect.

Ant. You would not let me read it, when y'have done?

Cæl. I do confess I should be loath, my Lord.
But yet from any Sin concerns your self,
I am as free as are the purer Angels,
Or may I find no profit by my Prayers.

Anto. I will believe thee; go, make haste and do it.

[Ex. Cælia.

Yet, if't be possible, I'm resolv'd to see it;
'Twill Cure my fears, perhaps, or change their Natures,
And make 'em certainties the lesser evil cause sooner Cur'd:
For Jealousies with fear doth plague the mind,
But that is Cur'd when certainties we find.

[Ex. Anto.

The Scene changes, Discovers Jasper, as from Bed, Buttoning himself.

Jasp. Oh, plague o'this Old Bitch, she has kept me so awake with her Coughing all Night, that I have quite out-slept my self.

[Looks on's Watch.

By Heav'n near Ten a Clock, and she not gone yet—plague on her—she'l be catch'd, and I shall be turn'd away—why Nurse—make haste, 'tis Ten a clock and past, you will be wanting.

Nurse within. That cannot be, alas, the times but short that I've been with thee, my Dear.

Jasp. No, perhaps you think so;
but let me ever want money to drink,
if I have not thought the time longer
then her Life has been, and that began beyond the mem'ry of man. What drudgery am I forc'd to undergo to get a little money to support me—that I may Live to watch all apted times for my Revenge on this whole family, who Rise upon the Ruines of our House.
7 This Nurse of Ninety never stayes with me but I'de as live have been Rid by a Night-Mare.

Enter Nurse.

Nurse. What's that, Night-Mare? Am I a Night-Mare?

Jasp. No, Nurse, I said, I was troubl'd with a Night-Mare, and should be worse, were it not for thy Company.

Nurse. Nay, I am good Friend of thine every way.

Jasp. That's true; but Nurse make haste, for I am damnably afraid *Flora* suspects us e're since she took me in your Chamber, and if she shou'd take you here, and tell my Lady, I should be turn'd away, for you know she loves me not e're since I gave my Lord notice of her meeting *Don Lewis*, to give him the money and Jewels, her Father left privately in her hands for him when he dy'd.

Nurse. I Chuck, but why didst thou do so?

Jasp. In hopes to have got some of the money for my discovery, what made her tempt me with the trust of money, and give me none to keep Counsel. But prethee Nurse be gone.

Nurse. I, give me but one buss, and I will.

[Kisses him, and is going.

Jasp. What a belch was there to perfume it?

[She comes back.

Nurse. Sweet Rogue, I cannot go without the other kiss.

Jasp. Oh, Nurse! you will undo me; prethee no more.

Nurse. What, Rascal, slight my favours? you shall repent it.

Jasp. No, Nurse, think not so, but—

Flora within.

Why, Nurse, Nurse, my Lady wants you; come away there, I know where you have been all Night.

Jasp. Why, there 'tis—this is what I fear'd, I am undone, a plague of Cubbard Love—step into the Closet.

Nurse. What's that you say, Cubbard Love?

Jasp. No, no, prethee no Arguments, but step into the Closet.

Flora within. Why, Nurse, I say! why don't you come away? My Lady wants you.

[Jasper goes to the Door.

Jasp. Flora, what's the matter with you? Nurse is not here; do but come in and see.

[Enter Flora.

8*Flor.* Come, come, she must be here; for she was not in her own Bed to Night, and where should she be, but with you?

Jasp. With me! what the Devil should she do with me? Can't her Old Chopps mumble her Beads o're, but I must keep count of her *Pater Nosters*: No, no, she's gon on Pilgrimage to some Shrine, to beg Children for my Lady; 'tis a devout Old Woman.

Flor. Devout! I, her Devotion and yours are much alike, the Fit ne're took you but once in your Lives, and then, 'tis true you wept at Prayers, that was, at your own Christnings.

Jasp. Prethee more Charity, sweet dear *Flora;* come, let me kiss thee.

Flor. Pray forbear, I'de sooner kiss a Horse.

Jasp. Why so scornful, dear *Flora*?

Flor. That's not my bus'ness; come, tell me, where's the Nurse?

Jasp. Prethee, why dost ask me for the Nurse? Dost think i am so hot to make Love to a Monument? Why, she's old enough to be Mother of all Mankind; her skin's turn'd to parchment, he that should enjoy her, had as good lye with a bundle of Old Records. In truth, she's fit for nothing now, but to be hang'd up amongst the monsters in a 'Pothecaries Shop, where, with abuse to the Beast, she would be taken for a large Apes skin stufft with Hay. Ah, *Flora,* if she were as Young as thou art, then't might be likely, I might find her when she was lost.

Flor. Well, if she be not here now, I'm sure it was not for nothing you once lost your way into her Chamber, and staid all Night.

Jasp. Meer Drunkenness, by this Light, *Flora*! Why, if it had been a Vault full of Dead Carkasses, I should have slipt into it in the pickle I was in—Nay, for ought I know, with more pleasure too.

[Enter Nurse.

Nurse. Now out upon you for a Rogue, there's no enduring this.

Jasp. Do but hear me, Nurse.

9C*Flor.* Ay, hear him, Nurse, he'l be sure to recant and swear you're as sweet as—a—fogh—so sweet—

Nurse. What, Hussy, dare you abuse me—I that gave suck to my Lady before thou wast born—you Young Whore.

Flor. Young Whore! why not Old Whore, Nurse, as well as young Whore?

Nurse. You damn'd Young Slut, I'le tear out your Eyes.

Flor. My Feet shall save my Eyes, except you can out-run me to my Lady.

[Exit Flora.

Jasp. Have not you made fine work now? I but dissembled to take off suspition—and you must shew your self, i'm sure I shall be turn'd away for your folly.

Nurse. But dissembled, said you? Marry, there's dissembling indeed.

Jasp. Nay, Nurse, consider, dost think I would have spoke so in thy hearing, had it been for any other thing? But prethee kiss me—I protest thou'rt as sweet as *Arsifettito.*

Nurse. Arsifettito! What's that?

Jasp. A Rich perfume the Chymists make, and good against fits o' th' Mother. But what shall I do now? I shall be turn'd away.

Nurse. I'le warrant thee, I'le place thee with *Eugenia,* she shall take care of thee for mine and a Friends sake of hers.

Jasp. Ay, ay, that's *Francisco;* but you have promis'd me often to tell me a secret concerns them; prethee do't now, Nurse.

Nurse. But will you ne're speak on't? If you do, I shall get no more money for thee, *Jasper;* that's the way, i get all, Chuck; no, no, no matter what's between them, trust thou to me.

Jasp. Well, Nurse, I thought you had Lov'd me, but I see you do not; you know I can keep secrets.

Nurse. Ay, but this is such a one I dare not tell it; besides, it was not *Eugenia*s fault at first—alas, poor fool, she was in a sad taking, when she found her Couzen *Francisco* in Bed with her.

Jasp. In Bed, sayst thou?

Nurse. Lord bless me! what have I done? If you should tell now.

Jasp. Ne're fear it, tell me all: I would not for the world have mist this Story, it makes a full amends for all my Crosses; come, Nurse, prethee quickly tell me all passages.

Nurse. I tell no more, my mind misgives me I've said too much already.

Jasp. Not tell me more, Old Beldame? Speak it quickly, or what I know shall soon unto my Lord.

Nurse. How now! Is this dissembling too?

Jasp. No, 'tis as great a truth as what you told me of, *Don Francisco*'s Bedding with *Eugenia;* tell me the rest, and by it save your Life.

Nurse. Dear *Jasper*, be not angry, and I will.

Jasp. Come, Nurse, do it, and then we'l kiss and be Friends. I shall have use of her.

[Aside.

Nurse. Now thou shalt have my heart; and thus it is: *Don Francisco* doth often meet *Eugenia* i'th' garden, who, to avoid suspition, after her Sisters in Bed, by my means gets her Night-Gown, and puts it on so to avoid being known, shou'd any see her.

Jasp. Oh, Excellent! when do they meet again?

Nurse. I've promis'd him this Night, though she was loath, till I told her he would but take his leave, for she's grown a little backward, now she's to marry *Don Gerardo.*

Jasp. Is she to marry him, sayst thou?

Nurse. I, sure, for he makes Love to her, and she's so hot upon't, that she vows after this Night never to meet *Francisco* any more; but I'le go Live with her, and so shalt thou.

Jasp. Ay, so I will—i'th' Garden, sayst thou, and in her sisters Gown, no body with them!

Nurse Yes, the Lord *Sebastian,* he knows all, and alwayes waits upon 'em.

Jasp. That's well, keep thou the secret close, and ne're fear me; but if my Lord should ask suspitiously questions 11C2 about his Wife—name *Pedro* to him, say, when he's from Home, that Fellow stayes too long within her chamber, and say, that *Flora* waits; leave me to prove it true.

Nurse. Why, 'tis not so, I dare not tell my Lord so damn'd a Lye.

Jasp. Why? Y'are a Fool, there shall no hurt come of it, only we'l be Reveng'd of *Pedro,* and that Slut, for they're our Enemies; besides, if you won't, I'le swear you told me so, and moreover, let him know all the rest y'have told me.

Nurse. Nay, don't be angry, and I'le do any thing.

Enter Cælia, Pedro, and Flora.

Cæl. Oh, thou Old doting Fool! what, still remain here! What punishment is proper for thy Age? As for you, Sirrah, I believe my Lord will find a way quickly to send you packing.

Jasp. It may be so, but 'tis without a cause.

Cæl. Impudent Villain! how I do hate thy sight. Follow you me.

[To Nurse.] [Ex. Cæl.Nurse, & Flora.

Ped. What, i'th' dumps, Seignior! all a mort for your mistress, faith man, take it not so to heart, there are others i'th' World as Young, though few may be as handsome.

Jasp. Ay, Sir, 'tis to be suppos'd; you can boast it by Experience, there are Young Ladies for spruce *Pedro's*—*Jasper*—must be content with their Nurses.

Ped. Content, say you? I, Marry, if she content you not, the Devil can't; why, she's a Dish of variety, like a huge *olio*; there's all Ages of Women in her. Thou art the happiest man in a Mistress, *Jasper*—faith, I envy thee.

Jasp. 'Tis very well.

Ped. Not too well neither.

Jasp. You may laugh; you stand on the top of Favour, have a care of falling down, I may catch you one day.

Ped. No, never with an Old Woman; it's worse then committing Incest; to Cuckold, for ought I know, a dozen Generations.

12*Jasp.* Rest you merry, I can leave you.

Ped. But I'le not quit you so.

[Exeunt.

Enter Antonio and Gerardo Discoursing.

Ger. In this dear Friend, consists my happiness;
Therefore deny me not—Why pause you, Sir?
My fears are come about—

Anto. What, hath *Eugenia* given her consent?

Ger. I say not so, my Lord, but her denyals
Were spoke so faintly, I Interpret well.

Anto. Dear Friend, I am afraid you do mistake
The Object of your Joyes, let me perswade
You to believe, there's not that happiness

In Marriage-Beds, as single People guess,
No, no, so far from that, that thousands be
Flatter'd by hopes to endless misery.
And where there's two obtain their hearts desire,
Ten thousand miss it, and in grief expire.

Ger. Were these Positions true, there's no man, sure,
If Widdowed once, could other Wives endure.
And yet we see the first depriv'd of Life,
There's few that seek not for a second Wife.

Anto. 'Tis true, though strange, but yet our minds are such,
As alwayes find too little, or too much;
Desire's a Monster, whose extended Maw
Is never fill'd, tho' it doth all things draw:
For we with envious Eyes do others see,
Who want our ills, and think they happy be,
Till we possessing what we wish'd before,
Find our ills doubl'd, and so wish for more.

Ger. Suppose all true which you wou'd have me fear,
Ills in possession still the greatest are:
And my desires to such a height do rise,
T' attain their ends, I shou'd all else despise.

Anto. Since y'are resolv'd, I'le not your ends deny,
But pray my words prove false when e're you try;
Though well they speak, who say the damned State,
Chiefly consists in wishing things too late:
13*Eugenia's* Father left her to my care,
Which trust to end so well I did despair:
Then name the day of Marriage—

*Ger.*No delay
My thoughts admit; I wish it were to day.

Anto. That cannot be, to Morrow I approve.

Ger. Time will flye slow, though Impt with wings of Love.

Enter Cælia and Eugenia.

Cæl. My Lord, I beg your pardon for a short interruption.

Ger. Madam, 'tis I have cause to beg your pardon,
Thus to detain your Lord, on's Wedding-day,
A Day in Justice should be wholly yours.

Cæl. My Lord is happy so to be detain'd
And I am alwayes happy when he's so.
Whispers Anto. he takes a paper privately out of her pocket. But good, my Lord, your Ear—

Ger. Madam, if you repent not what y'have said,
In answer to those Vows of my Affection,
I then dare hope I may in time be happy.

Eugen. Tho' I ne're thought your words were further means,
Then to pass time away in Raillery;
Yet were my Answers such, as if you had
Told me a real Story of your Love:
And the same Answers I'le again renew;
My Will's confin'd; my Fathers last Commands
Left me no Choice but anothers will;
If I were free, I then durst speak my thoughts:
But I, in all, my Brother must obey.

Ger. He checks your Actions only, thoughts are free,
Suppose him willing, would you favour me?

Eugen. But to suppose without his Will's a Crime,
If I that supposition should declare.

Ger. I do confess I should be loath to own
That Blessing which I rate above my Life,
If 'twere bestow'd by any hands but yours;
Therefore by all your hopes I do conjure you,
If you dislike my Love, Command my silence.

Eugen. Interpret well my blushes, when I say
14 I cannot find a thought for such Commands.

Ger. Then I am happy 'bove the reach of Envy;
For I have his consent already granted,
He nam'd the day of Marriage as you enter'd.

Eugen. You see, my Lord, that I had cause for fear,
Since I'm bestow'd, and my consent ne're askt.
Sure my dead Father ne're design'd it so?

Ger. Madam, I beg your pardon, for a truth
Might well excuse your Brother in this matter;
I urg'd to him I doubted not your favour,
On which Condition he did grant me his.

Eugen. I shall hear further of it from himself,
Till when, I beg your pardon.

[Offers to go out.

Anto. Sister, pray stay, for I have bus'ness with you.
I know, my Dear, you never Lov'd that Fellow,
Which since you do not, though he serves me well,
Yet I'm resolv'd for this to part with him,
Tho' I could think a Pension for your Nurse,
To keep her at a distance, were as well.

Cæl. Though now her dotage makes her want discretion,
Her Love to us was great.

Anto. Come, trouble not your self about it, he shall go.

Cæl. My Lord, I'le trouble you no further.

Ger. I'le wait upon you, Madam.

[Ex. Gerar. and Cæl.

Anto. Sister, you know your Father was my Friend,
And was so confident that I was his,
He trusted all your Fortunes in my hands,
Though he had Brothers Living when he Dy'd,
He told you too, and left it in his Will,
That what you had was mine, if you did Marry
Without my Approbation: Is't not true?

Eugen. Sir, 'tis a truth I'm glad of.

Anto. These things your Kindred though, did call contrivance,
Which made their hatred rise so much against me,
It makes a few'd betwixt our Families,

Which soon would come to Blood, but for Respect
They bear my Wife, their Cozen.

Eugen. Brother, I cannot answer for their Actions,
My own Respects to you were never wanting.

Anto. I do not deny it, Sister; and to prove
I never did, nor will deserve worse from you,
If you are willing now to change your State,
And know a man preferr'd in your Election,
Let him have Blood and worth, you and your Fortune
I freely will resign into his hands.
Then truly speak your thoughts.

*Eugen.*Surely, my Lord,
You'd scarcely think I should be worth your care,
If I should choose before you nam'd one to me.

Anto. Sister, I see your Kindreds Jealousies
Partly infects you too; but to remove them,
What think you of *Gerardo*, for a Husband?
My wishes meet with yours, if he's their Object;
You know I'm no Dissembler.

Eugen. Nor shall you find me so; for I confess
In this you prove your Kindness, Care, and Justice;
And I must meet it with my greatest thanks.

Anto. I'm joyful for it; to morrow is the day,
A private Wedding will prevent all Rumour,
You'd best withdraw then to provide your self.

[Ex. Eugen.

What Paper's this I got out of her Pocket?
Pray Heaven it be the right; it is the same,
The very same — — what makes me tremble!
Is't horror or desire, or both assault me?
Be it what it will, 'tis Hell to live in doubt;
But stay, my Conscience sayes 'tis Sacriledge —
What's that? A word by cunning Priests invented
To keep the Cheats they live by from our knowledge;
As the *Ægyptian* did with *Hieroglyfficks;*

But be it what it will, a Name, or thing,
I'le read it, for't may Cure my Jealousie,
And surely that exceeds Hells misery.
But to my Closet, where no Eye can see,
All are call'd Pious, who live scandal free.

[Exit.

16 Enter Eugenia and Nurse.

Eugen. Since he has promis'd but to take his leave,
And neither then, nor never urge more Sin,
I am content to give him this last meeting.

Nurse. He'l be a glad man, I'm sure—but what shall poor *Jasper* do?

Eugen. If he will marry you, I'le keep you both.

Nurse. Thank you, Madam, I'le tell him your good will.

[Exit.

Eugen. What by this cursed Sin am I reduc'd to?
To be a Slave to Slaves; nay, worse, a Bawd,
A Name so base, profest ones do detest it,
And yet I'm one, this cursed Hellish Hagg has made me so.
The first did sell, and then betray'd my Honour,
Yet thinks she has oblig'd me by the Action.
Nay, I am forc't to say so now to please her;
Some heavenly Angel make me Chaste again,
Or make me nothing, I am resolv'd to try,
Before I'de still live Whore, I'de choose to dye.

Enter Jasper.

Jasp. I'm come to thank your Lady-ship for the great care,
Nurse sayes, you have of me; but faith, Madam, I
was ne're made to be Steel to a Tinder-Box; she's
meer Touch-wood; no, I'm not for Marrying great
grannums: But if your Lady-ship knows any Young
Dame, that wants a strong back to do her drudgery,
though it be in her Lord's absence, I'm content.

Eugen. What, is the Fellow mad?

Jasp. No, Madam, not mad at all, but can as soberly keep councel as the best Young Gallant of 'em all; and am as able to do the feat: Please your Lady-ship to try me, and praise me as you find; if you dislike my work, I'le lose my labour, and have nothing for my pains.

Eugen. Oh, strange, unheard-of Impudence! Out, Villain.

[Ex.

Jasp. So scornful! Villain! Nay, if you call me so, 'tis time
to be so; what a Devil ayls my face, that she contemns
me thus? May be my Nose is not long enough she thinks,
pox on her Pride, 'tis that or'e-comes her Leachery—I must
17D alter my Trade, for I was ne're born I see to thrive by
love; then I'le set up a shop of hatred, and the Wares I
vent shall be Revenge, that may hit; but hold, my Lord.

Enter Antonio.

Anto. What have I got? Am I more satisfy'd
By this same Paper then I was before?
No, not at all; and yet why should I not?
There's not a thought set down concerneth me—
Yet that's her policy—
She either fear'd that I should get the Paper,
Or else on purpose did contrive I might;
But how can I know that? This Jealousie,
If it continue long, will make me mad.

Jasp. Well, the Devil has put him on this pin meerly to do me a kindness.

Anto. And yet it must continue, who can Cure it?
Ay, there's it, who can Cure it? Then I must be mad!
Nay, I'm mad already, stark mad!—

Jasp. My good Lord.

Anto. What's the matter? I fear he heard me.

[Aside.

Jasp. I come to take leave of your Lordship, I have enemies I hear have turn'd me going.

Anto. Is't not deservedly, thou Goat?

Jasp. Yes, yes, it may be so, since they will have it so; but if I had never seen, I had ne're been turn'd away for doing: If I were as ready to make mischief, as I am fear'd to be; Nurse and I had not been only the Sufferers.

Anto. Explain your Riddle, Sirrah.

Jasp. Nay, let my Tongue come out e're I say any thing to disquiet your Lordship, I love you better.

Anto. Disquiet me! What lyes within thy power to say that can disquiet me?

Jasp. Nay, nothing it may be, my Lady is my Lady, and you are a kind Lord, that's all I know; so begging your Lordships Discharge, I'm gone, and then their Fears are over.

18*Anto.* Villain, thou'st given me poyson; my veins swell with it, produce the Antidote, or I'le dissect thy Soul to find it out; what is't you know that can disquiet me?

Jasp. I know little, my Lord, to' th' purpose, besides, it will but vex you, since there may be no harm in it.

Anto. Come, come, no going back, tell quickly what you know.

Jasp. I know, why, I know that my Lady hates me, because I told your Lordship the time she was to deliver the Jewels and Money to *Don Lewis*, and still she calls me false in being true to you—but—

Anto. But what?

Jasp. But if I should say all I know—well, but let that alone, good, my Lord, your Discharge.

Anto. Vile Dog, dost raise my Anger for to play with it? I'le vent it upon thee then.

[Draws, and cuts at him.

Jasp. Hold, hold, my Lord, and I'le tell all I know.

Anto. Let's hear it.

Jasp. When you lay hid about *Don Lewis*'s death, I've
often seen a Lady in the Night to meet two Men
i'th' Garden, but am not sure it was your Lady.

Anto. What makes you name her then?

Jasp. Her Gown, I think it was her Gown.

Anto. Wa'st often, say you?

Jasp. Yes, every Night, except you lay at home, for I
took pains to watch, they never fail'd coming,
but there was but one of them went into the House,
Sir, and he neither would not stay above an hour
at most: this is all.

Anto. All, quoth a! What Devil would have more,
if 'twas my Lady.

Jasp. I can't say that, but yet I dare be sworn it was
her Gown, I do believe, I mean, I think it was.

Anto. Could you not guess the men?

Jasp. I think they were *Francisco* and *Sebastian*.

Anto. It must be they; a plague upon their Fewds;
They can Revenge themselves upon my Wife:
Go, call the Nurse, this she must needs conspire in;
19D2 But keep all private from her.

[Exit Jasper.

Is she so bucksome? Has she more Kinsmen Stallions?
I'le cleanse her Blood, or empty all her veins;
confessions calls she these! Betwixt Religion and her Leachery
the Devil dances Barley-break—but hold—why
may'nt the Rogue contrive this for Revenge?
For if I reflect his pretending not to tell, did but
usher in the Story. I must be cautious of a too light belief.

Enter Cælia.

Cæl. My Lord, by Accident I've lost a Paper, which troubles me.

Anto. A Paper, say you? I took up one i'th' Garden, and I think this is it.

Cæl. It is, my Lord, and I rejoyce no other Person found it.

Anto. Why, what is it?

Cæl. 'Tis the Confession that I told you of.

Anto. I might have read it then, and ne're askt you, had I but known it.

Cæl. If your Lordship pleases you may read it.

Anto. No, no, I will not, but prethee keep it better.

Cæl. My Lord, there are some Tenants, who desire to express their Loves by Rural Recreations—

Anto. Bid e'm stay, their sports are more in season after Dinner. So willing now to have it read, and yet before so backward!

[Ex. Cæl.

Why, this confirms me she is false, it was contriv'd on purpose for my sight. The Devil's not so cunning as a Woman.

[Enter Nurse.

Oh, Beldame, are you come? Tell me, you Bawd,
Who Whores my Wife? For Whore I know she is,
And you're her Bawd. Tell me, I say, the man,
The place, the Circumstance, and very time,
Or I will quarter thee, and throw thy flesh to'th' dogs.

Nurse. Alas, my Lord, I know nothing, but that when you're from Home, *Pedro* goes to her Chamber, and stays there all Night, but what they do, I know not, for none but *Flora's* with them.

Anto. Pedro! Oh monstrous, she would devour a Legion! Is't every Night, do you say?

Nurse. Yes, every Night; but I durst never tell you!
Alas, she suckt these Breasts.

Anto. Shew me this Night *Pedro*, in Bed with her,
or I will cut thy Tongue out.

Nurse. 'Tis impossible when you are at home.

Anto. I will contrive a Journey out of Town, but will at
twelve return, then let me in; for if you fail
I'le cut your Throat.

Nurse. I'le do my best.

[Exit.

Anto. Pedro! What sordid Devil prompted her to that?
Why, I am known to all the World a Cuckold;
The very Boys i'th' street must point at me;
But hold, this new Intelligence struck out the old,
And made me quite forget about *Francisco*.

Enter Jasper.

Oh, *Jasper*! I'm confirm'd my Wife's a Devil,
And I will send her to the rest e're Morning;
Go and contrive a Letter from *Don John;*
Shall intimate he's sick, and wants my presence,
Then I'le contrive the rest.

Jasp. Be not too rash, my Lord, might I advise
You should be certain e're you Acted ought.

Anto. How can I be more certain then this Night,
To be Eye-witness of her Lust my self,
As Nurse has undertook I shall.

Jasp. Ay, Sir, but things may fail, and they not meet.

Anto. Name a more certain way then.

Jasp. My Lord, there lives a Woman in the Suburbs,
Mighty in Science, who by Art can tell
All that she pleases, I'de have you go to her.

Anto. Is she of your acquaintance?

Jasp. No, my Lord, she scorns such things as me,
She's for the great ones; though for Charity,
She sometimes helps poor people to their goods,
I'me sure she'd serve your Lordship.

Anto. I fear she'l never trust us, lest we should betray
Her to the Inquisition.

21*Jasp.* No fear of that, she cannot be betray'd,
She knows Mens bus'ness er'e they come unto her.

Anto. Well then, contrive my absence, I'le go thither,
I'm sure to know whether she cheats or no,
For if she names *Don Lewis* 'mongst the rest,
I shall believe her. Well, about the Letter.

[Exit.

Jasp. Are you there with your Beares; *Don Lewis* say you?
Marry now I find 'twas Jealousie of his Wife;
and not the matter of Money made him kill him,
whether he was guilty or no; I'le be sure he shan't
be forgot, for I'le before hand to my Aunt, and tell
her all; I hope, she is a Witch; the People say so, a
mighty Artist I am sure she is, for she has done
strange things, and all men fear her, besides I
know she loves me, and will strive all she can to
do me good, and hap what will my Lord will
think me honest; for Night will surely shew his
sister to him, drest in's Ladyes Gown, what though
he kill her, the mistake will lye o'th' Night, and not
on me, thus I make good the Villain that she call'd
me, in my Revenge on her; and if Nurse fails me
not, I'le have my Lady, and *Pedro*; finely firkt.
When this is done, my Lord rewards my care,
Let him the danger I'le the profit share.
And since things Excellent commended be,
'Tshall be my Aym t'excell in Villany.

The End of the first Act.

22

Act the Second.

Enter Jasper and the Witch.

Jasp.
THis kindness, Aunt, I beg, your Art must do;
For I have no way else to save my place.

Witch. Why, 'tis impossible; I've no such Art
As People think, to call up Spirits to me;
Nor know I any thing, but what is told me.

Jasp. Now you dissemble, Aunt, for han't you often
Rais'd Storms, have rent up Trees, and shook strong
Towers? Seeming to threaten Nature with it's end;
And at such times have sent strange shaped
Spirits, who have restored to owners stolen Goods.
These things so many know, it is impossible
For you to keep it private; but I find,
Rather then trust me with your mighty secrets,
Or help me with your Art, you'l see my Ruine.

Witch. These things you speak of, people think I do,
And so I'de have e'm; for tis the only way I have to Live:
The Vulgar People love to be deluded;
And things the most unlikely they most dote on;
A strange Disease in Cattle, Hogs or Pigs,
Or any Accident in Cheese or Butter;
Though't be but Natural, or a Sluts fault,
Must strait be Witchcraft! Oh, the Witch was here!
The Ears or Tail is burn'd, the Churn is burn'd;
And this to hurt the Witch, when all the while
They're likest Witches that believe such Cures;
Could I do all that People think I can,
I'de ne're take pains to find out stolen Goods,
23 Or hold intelligence with Thieves to bring e'm,
Meerly to get my Bread; no, I would make
The Universe pay Tribute to my power,
And all the Bug-bear Lords Inquisitors
More tremble at my Name then I do now
At theirs: Ah, *Jasper*, would I raise

Storms when I would, blast Corn, turn Rivers backward
Change shapes, mov'd where I pleas'd i'th' Air,
And that so fast, as thought it self would
Hardly overtake me:
What is't I could not do? if all were true
The Foolish People think, the Pope himself would
Quickly lose Respect,
And none be thought infallible but I.

Jasp. I'm sure I tremble for your want of power,
More then I should to see Hells dreadfull'st shape,
For I must flye the Town.

Witch. Jasper, not so; though I can raise no Devils,
Yet I Confederate with Rogues and Juglers,
Things that can shape themselves like Elves,
And Goblins—
And often do like Spirits haunt great Houses,
Most times to steal, but many times for mirth;
Enter a little Devil, and tumbles the Summerset. These I'le soon send for; arise, my *Pincula*.

Jasp. Heav'ns bless me! save me, good Aunt.

Witch. From what? You Fool, 'tis but a little Boy,
Which I instruct to carry on my Cheats:
Come, leave your Fooling, I have bus'ness for you;
Uncase your self, and quickly go and find
Ranter, and *Swash*, *Dive*, *Fob*, *Snap*, *Gilt*, and *Pick-lock*,
Those are my Archest Devils; as you go
Call upon *Dog'rell* the Ballad-maker, and say
I want him strait, bid them be sure
To bring home half a dozen more with them,
For I shall need their help, let e'm not fail,
For money's to be got.

Devil. 'Tis that will make e'm come; I'le haste, forsooth.

[Exit.

24*Jasp.* I'm glad it's gone, for surely it was a Devil,
What ever you pretend.

*Witch.*Thou'rt a Fool:
It was a Boy, I tell thee, and no Devil;
Nor am I a sorceress, though I could wish
To do thee good I was: But 'tis no matter,
Bring thou thy Lord, I'le practice well enough
To make him think all true, that I shall shew him.

Jasp. You now Revive my Drooping Spirits, Aunt, and
Make my hopes grow strong! Ah sweet Revenge,
How my soul Dances but with thoughts of it;
Assist me, Aunt, to get this mighty Blessing, and I
Shall dye your slave.

Witch. O rare Boy!
How I rejoyce to see this Spirit in thee,
For 'tis the vertue of our Family
To seek Revenge, not basely swallow wrongs:
Don Sancho De Mensalvo, thy Grandsire
Was for a while Vice-Admiral of Spain,
But then disgrac'd turn'd Pyrate and Reveng'd
With Fire and Sword on all Mankind, the wrongs
He thought the Court had basely plac'd on him;
At last he was betray'd and lost his head,
Thy Father turn'd Bandetto, what he got
I did dispose of for him; but his Fate
Betray'd him too to Death by Execution:
Since when I by these Arts do strive to live,
And thou art forc'd to serve—
That very Lord, who does those Lands
Possess should have been thine.

Jasp. But will e're long mount to some higher sphere,
Or dye in the attempt; this Plot, perhaps, may do,
And I thereby obtain some part of my Estate
Again; for if the plotted mischiefs shall succeed,
I'le tell him whom I am, and my resolves, either
To share his Fortunes or Reveal all. Then I will
Rise *Don Jasper De Monsalvo* and Cheek by Jole,
25E Ask how *Antonio* does. Then don't forget the names.

Witch. Not one of them: I know them very well.

Jasp. Farewell, Dear Aunt, but don't you seem to know me.

Witch. Out you great Fool! What become my Instructer?
Be careful of your self, and fear not me. Farewel, boy.

[Exeunt.

Enter Antonio, Gerardo, Cælia, Eugenia, as to a Masque, and take their seats.

Ger. Have you heard, Madam, what they represent?

Cælia My Lord, I'm told they mean to play the Gipsies,
And tell our fortunes to us.

*Anto.*I would they could.

Eugen. If all Man's life determin'd is before,
I would not know my Destiny me-thinks,
For good is best, when least it is Expected;
And bad fore-seen is doubl'd by our fear
Things certain no fore-knowledge can prevent
Such knowledge only can bring discontent.

Ger. In this with you I perfectly agree.

Anto. Yet for all that I wish I could foresee.

Cælia. My Lord, what profit by it wou'd you gain?

Anto. 'Twould cure doubt to me the deadliest pain.

Ger. Doubt is th'effect of fear or Jealousie,
Two Passions which to Reason give the Lye
For fear torments, but never does assist,
And Jealousie is love lost in a Mist.
Both Hood-wink truth, then go to blind-mans buff,
Cry here, then there, seem to direct enough:
But all the while shift place making the mind
As it goes out of breath despair to find.
And if at last something it stumbles on,
Perhaps it calls it false and then 'tis gone.
If true, what's gain'd only just time to see
A breachless Play a Game at Liberty;

That has no other end then this, that men
Run to be tyr'd just to set down agen.

Anto. This is a truth, and so for ought I know,
To the same purpose tends all things we do:
26 Life's a Disease, and yet we seldom say,
That Man is sick whom we see laugh and play;
And 'tis as well to bid the Bed-rid ride,
As to bid Men in doubt be satisfy'd:
For 'tis the mind's Disease, and Physick should
Be proper to't, or else the Patient's fool'd.
And there's no Drug in Nature doubt to Cure
But only one, and that is to be sure.

Cæl. Yes, Circumstance, my Lord, if well apply'd.

Anto. I've known that often fail, when it was try'd
But they come—

[Flourish.

Enter first Gipsie, and sings.

1. Gipsie.
COme, come, away; follow, follow your Prince,
I am King of the swarthy Complexions;
Follow me that can lead you through Chimneys and Chinks
To steal Bacon and Pease;
Nay, sometimes with ease
To a Feast of the choycest Confections.
Come, follow me then, come away, come away.

Enter second Gipsie, and sings.

2. Gip. We know no Rebellion, but obey, but obey,
To our King we are just,
And true to our trust,
Leaving discord to those, that their Princes oppose,
When by the Spirit of Treason in Non-sence they pray.

Enter all the rest, and sing.

Chor. We know &c.

1. Gip. Come then, and follow, a prize, a prize, a prize.

2. Gip. Give the word then, and helloa.

All. A prize, a prize, a prize.

27E21. Gip. Here are Gallants and Ladies have fortunes to tell.

2. Gip. We'l tell e'm good Fortune if they give us a spell.

1. Gip. A hand crost with silver the Spirit infuses.

2. Gip. There's no Prophet lately that mettle refuses.

1. Gip. Men get Heaven now by Bargain and Sale.
Masses, Trentals and Dirges
Are not had for no Charges,
And a Vicar for nothing won't tell you a Tale.

All. Masses, &c.

1. Gip. All things are bought and sold.

2. Gip. Good Fortune goes with Gold.

1. Gip. Fall on to your Trading then.

Men Gip. W'are for the Ladies.

Wom. Gip. And we for the Men.

1. Gip. To *Cæl.* Lady, you have lost a Lover,
Cross my hand, I'le more discover.

2. Gip. To *Anto.* My Lord, I know you baseness scorn,
And would be loath to wear a Horn.

1. Gip. To *Eug.* Lady, some do speak you fair,
That hatred to your welfare bear.

2. Gip. To *Ger.* My Lord, you Love a handsom Lady,
She Loves you as well it may be.

1. Gip. sings. Thus we seldom miss the matter,
Things past we can tell, by these Generals well,
And ne're stay to prove the truth of the latter.

All. Things past, &c.

1. To *Cæl.* You shall Live long and happily, Lady.

2. To *Anto.* My Lord, I can tell you, good Fortunes your Friend.

1. To *Eug.* You shall e're long play with your own Baby.

2. To *Ger.* Your Love my Lord, will have good end.

1. Gip. sings. Thus we Live merrily, merrily, merrily,
And thus to our Dancing we sing;
Our Lands and our Livings
Lye in others believings,
When to all Men we tell the same thing:
And thus to our Dancing we sing.
Thus we, &c.

[An Antique of Gipsies, and Exeunt.

28*Anto.* By this we see that all the Worlds a Cheat,
Where truths and falshoods lye so intermixt,
And are so like each other, that 'tis hard
To find the difference; who would not think these People
A real pack of such as we call Gipsies.

Ger. Things perfectly alike are but the same;
And these were Gipsies, if we did not know
How to consider them the contrary;
So in Terrestial things there is not one
But takes its Form and Nature from our fancy;
Not its own being, and is what we do think it.

Anto. But truth is still it self.

Ger. No, not at all, as truth appears to us;
For oftentimes
That is a truth to me that's false to you,
So 'twould not be if it was truly true.

Enter Pedro *and a Servant, with a Letter to* Antonio.

Serv. My Lord, *Don John* salutes you in that Letter.

Cæl. How does my Couzen, Friend?

Serv. Madam, I fear he's drawing near his end.

Cæl. 'Pray Heav'n divert it.

Anto. The Letter shews, that Death did guide his hand;
It only says, Oh Friend, come now or never.

Ger. How did his Sickness take him?

Serv. Chacing the Buck too hard; he hot with Labour,
Drunk of a cooling Spring too eagerly,
And that has given him pains, the Doctors say,
Will give him Death immediately.

Cæl. Heav'n grant him help.

Anto. Return, and tell thy Lord, I'm at thy heels.
Pedro, bring my Boots, and bid two Horses be made ready.

Cæl. Whom do you take, my Lord?

Anto. Pedro:—but hold, *Jasper* is not discharg'd, I'le ee'n take him.

Cæl. Jasper, my Lord! Pray take not him.

Enter Ped.
with Boots.*Anto.* Why not him, there are no Nurses there?
29 Where's *Jasper Pedro*?

Ped. He said he wou'd not dine, and went abroad, yet I suppose he may be now in's Chamber.

Anto. Reach my Bootes, who has worn 'em lately?
I do believe you get into my Bootes.

Strikes Pedro with a Boot'top.*Ped.* I, my Lord.

Anto. I, you, my Rogue! Go, see for *Jasper*.

[Exit Pedro.

Cæl. My Lord! Why do you thus disturb your self?

Anto. You see the blow don't maim him, you need not be concern'd.

Cælia. What means my Lord?

Anto. As you hate *Jasper*, I hate whom I please.

Enter Jasper.

Cæl. His sight strikes terror to me!

Anto. Jasper, make ready, you must go with me.

[Exit Jasp.

Cæl. Here on my knees I beg you would not take him:
But if you be resolv'd, let me go too.

Anto. That cannot be: Don *John's* a Batchellor,
And is not fitted to have Women guests.

Cæl. I will dispence with any thing, my Lord,
Then let me go, or do not take *Jasper*.

Anto. Come, I must break this Childish way of yours,
Jasper shall go, and you shall stay at home,
And so Farewell; make merry with our Friends.

Ger. Do not resolve, my Lord; see how she takes it.

Anto. This passion soon will over; farewell, Friend,
I shall return to give *Eugenia* to you.

[Exit Anto.

Ger. I ne're perceiv'd his will to reign before,
Some sudden fancy makes him Obstinate.

Eug. So, give her Air, she comes to her self.

Cæl. Where is my Lord! What gone! am I deluded?
I Saw an Angel lead him back again.

Ger. Her fancy is disturb'd, make no answer:

Cæl. Why Sister, where's my Lord?

Eug. Do not disturb your self, my Brother's well.

Cæl. Get me a horse, for I will follow him.

Enter Antonio Bleeding.

Anto. Fetch me some water there.

Cæl. My Dream was true, my Dearest Lord's return'd!
What makes you Bleed?

Anto. As I was lifting up my Foot to the Stirrop, my Nose
Gusht out a Bleeding.

Eugen. My Sister dreamt, an Angel led you back,
And I believe it now.

Ger. Pray take some other with you, I, if you please
Will keep you Company.

Ant. No, I'm resolv'd to stay, and send him word, I am
Took ill my self; my Nose leaves Bleeding.

Cæl. I am satisfy'd, my Lord, you do not go, and therefore
Will Retire.

[Ex. all but Anto. and Gerar.

*Anto.*Do so, my Dear.
Now I must tell my Friend, I dare not stay,
Twould look but ill to say a Bleeding Nose
Made *Don Antonio* slight his dying Friend.

Ger. If that was all, it would; but yet reflect
There are more Prodigies forbid this Journey
Then *Cæsar* had t'avoyd the Senate-House.

Anto. Had *Cæsar* not been slain, those Accidents
We now call Prodigies, had been forgot;
And so will these when I am safe return'd.

Ger. Consider but your Ladies high concern,
Her suddain sounding, and recovery,
On which she cry'd an Angel brings him back,
Your Bleeding and Return speaks the dream't true,
The stopping of it too was not the least,
All these together force me to believe
That you from heav'n these warnings did receive.

Anto. Surely, *Gerardo*, we must heav'n offend
To think that it these Accidents should send.
It is detraction to the Pow'rs above,

To think they suffer what they don't approve,
For if they did this to divert my ill,
They go about, for they might change my will.
31 But mine's more firm; nay, more, should I not go,
The threaten'd ill I meet, for ought I know;
For if their boads be certain, then I may
Meet th' effects whether I go or stay.

Ger. Vainly we speak of heav'n, when vainly we
By human Wit set Rules to heav'ns decree,
The pow'r that made us gave us scope of will,
Freely to take the good, or choose the ill:
And though it can, it does not change that course,
Only perswades to Act what it could force.

Anto. This you believe, but you must pardon me,
If in this point I don't with you agree;
For if to Man such a free-will be given,
That damns all Præscience and so baffles heav'n:
But I delay whilst Reason bids me go,
And Reason 'tis, since it to me is so,
Then pray divert my Wife, so farewell, Friend.

[Exit.

Ger. Farewell: May all my fears to nothing tend;
Yet still I fear what should the Reason be,
That I shou'd fear, yet nothing fearful see,
I am resolv'd to send some Servants out
Shall wait him at a distance;
In doing all I can, I do the best,
I can no more, let heav'n do the rest.

[Exit.

Enter Don Francisco and Nurse.

Fran. Well, 'tis so sweet a sin to Wench in danger, that I am like to lose the best part of my Recreation; but prethee Nurse, tell me, what causes this change?

Nurse. Now if I would be hang'd, I cannot forbear telling. Faith, my Lord, *Gerardo*'s like to be the Man now, though I am for your Lordship still, you're my best Friend.

Fran. By heav'n I'le be his Death, and hers to boot;
can she slight me for him, he Whore our Kindred!
When did he first enjoy her?

Nurse. Not so, my Lord, he's to Marry her.

Fran. Nay, if't be so; then I'm Reveng'd already,
For's joyning with *Antonio* 'gainst our house,
32 He's Antidated Cuckold, and by me!
O rare Revenge! There's for thy News, Nurse.

[Gives money to her.

Were all my Enemies but serv'd the same;
At a more full Revenge I'de never aim.

Nurse. Me-thinks you should not be so merry for losing my Lady; 'faith, had I known it, you should not have come into the place you wot'on, by my means.

Fran. Nay, be not angry, Nurse, I find her drift.
She loves our family, and studies to Revenge it.
To make him Cuckold; how it pleases me!
Poyson, nor Poniards is not half so well,
Go, tell her; Nurse I'm glad she takes this way:
I glory in her love! by Heaven I do,
I'le find Sebastian out, and laugh with him,
Till I e'en split my sides.

Nurse. Sir, you'le tell no body I hope.

Fran. No, none but him:
To say as he goes by, there goes my Cuckold;
And then to laugh, go Nurse, and tell her
I'le be sure to meet—

[Exit.

Nurse. Another double Pistoll for my *Jasper*!
I'le have him one whole night for this.

For to speak truth, I find the Rogue does not love me:
Heavens! What a bad world is this,
an Old Woman, though never so willing,
can scarce get a friend for ready money:
when such as *Eugenia* can make the Gold fly about;
but time will come she must be fain to turn tail,
and pay for one as I do, or go without.
But it pleases me, my Lady says, he shall be my husband,
then I shall need give money no longer: for faith if he
be negligent, I'le ring him a Peal to quicken him to his duty.
thus marry'd once, I'le doe like other wives
that make their husbands drudge for quiet lives.

The End of the Second Act.

33F

Act the Third.

Enter Don Gerardo with a Book in his Hand.

Song.

1.

SOme Happy Soul come down and tell
What Joys are those with you do dwell?
If it be Happiness like ours below,
Which from our want of ills does only flow,
Then 'tis plain that mighty theam
Of Immortality is but a Dream.

2.

'Tis Love, 'tis Love, for nothing can
Give real Happiness to Man,
But Joys like those that Lovers Souls enjoy,
which here on Earth there's nothing can destroy;
Ay, ay, 'tis Love only can be
The Happy Souls endless felicity.

Ger. What a dull, heavy load hangs on my soul!
Weighing me down to Earth, as if 'twould say
'Twas weary of its Burthen, and resolv'd
To shake it off, and mix with its first matter;
What is the thing, call'd Death, we mortals shun?
Is't some real, or is't a fancy only?
Like that imaginary point in Mathematicks;
Not to be found only in definition:
It is no more: Death, like your Childrens Bug-bears,
Is fear'd by all, yet has no other Being
Then what weak fancy gives it; 'tis a Line,
34 But yet imaginary, drawn betwixt
Time and that dreadful thing Eternity;
I, that's the thing, 'tis fear'd; for now I find it:
Eternity which puzzles all the World,
To name the inhabitants that People it:
Eternity, whose undiscover'd Countrey
We Fools divide, before we come to see it;
Making one part contain all happiness,
The other misery, then unseen fight for't.
Losing our certains for uncertainties;
All Sects pretending to a Right of choyce;
Yet none go willingly to take their part,
For they all doubt what they pretend to know,
And fear to mount, lest they should fall below:
Be't as it will; my Actions shall be just,
And for my future State I Heav'n will trust.

Enter a Servant.

Return'd already; what can be the cause?

Serv. Sir, *Don Antonio* likewise is return'd.

Ger. What reason had he for it, dost thou know?

Ser. My Lord, I do not; for we by your appointment
Having took Horse, did with our greatest speed
Pursue the Road should lead us to *Don John*'s;
When near a Thicket stands some two Miles off,
I spy'd *Antonio* lying on the ground,

And *Jasper* walking of the Horses by him,
Fearing his seeing us, we took the Thicket,
Where shelter'd from their Eyes, I left my Fellows.
But I approach'd as near as possible,
Hoping I did you Service, if I could
By their Discourse gather their cause of stay.

Ger. 'Twas like thy self, both diligent and prudent.

Serv. But all my care did signifie but little,
The Wind blew fresh, and rustling in the Wood,
Wholly destroy'd their Voyces, so that few words
Of what they said I heard; and those I did,
Came so divided they had no connexion.

35F2*Ger.* What sort of Actions did you then perceive?

Serv. My Lord, I saw *Antonio* much disturb'd;
Sometimes he'd rise and walk a turn or two
With eager pace, then stop as suddenly,
Then stamp and tear his hair; then loudly cry.
She's dead, she's dead! Oh, *Cælia*, Oh, *Antonio*!
Then lye him down again, and rest a space:
Sometimes call *Jasper* to him, talk a while,
And soon again rise in another Passion;
Seldom I heard a word, except a Curse!
Or now and then a Name; as *Lewis*, *Cælia*,
Pedro, *Francisco*, *Flora*; nay, my Lord,
Sometimes I heard your Name, and then *Eugenia's*;
Then suddenly holding his hands to Heav'n,
He'd down again, and there a while would role.

Ger. These Actions sure did seem a perfect madness.

Serv. It seem'd indeed a madness methodiz'd,
Like theirs who are Transported far with Passion.

Ger. But how perceiv'd you *Jasper* bear himself?

Serv. Quite in another manner, but as strange!
For when his Lord look'd down, his looks would be
As full of mirth, ready to burst in Laughter;
That I perceiv'd he scarce contain'd himself:

But if his Lord did look about to speak,
Then was his Face demure, with hand on Breast,
Turning his Eyes to Heav'n, and groaning sighs.
As you have seen, my Lord, a Canting Preacher
Aiming to cheat his Audience, wanting matter,
Sigh to seem Holy, till he thought on something.
So at that distance seem'd his Actions to me;
But when his back was turn'd, the Rascal would
Make Mouths, and point with signs of greatest scorn.

Ger. There is some Fatal Villany in this;
Some Mystery beyond my Fathoming:
But how long staid they thus?

Serv. About two hours, when mounting both their Horses,
I took mine, and un-espy'd did dogg e'm to the City,
36 And where they Hous'd I know not; for they enter'd
Remote from Home, and I i'th' streets soon lost e'm.

Ger. Do both your Fellows know this?

*Serv.*No, my Lord,
I did not think it would become my Duty
To tell them any thing but what they saw.

Ger. I never knew thee yet mistake thy trust;
Thy secrecy was well: Preserve it still,
For I must use it further, therefore go,
And Charge your Pistols, we must walk a Round
About *Antonio*'s House to watch their motion;
For there the Scene must lye of this design;
If there be mischief in't, thy courage now
(If theirs occasion) must again be try'd.
And well Rewarded too.

Serv.'Tis so, my Lord,
Above all other wayes in that you trust it.
But I'le be gone, and Execute your Orders.

[Exit.

Ger. A Faithful Servant is the best of Friends,
Since he is nearest alwayes to assist us;

But stay, I cannot guess from all I've heard,
The cause that should disturb *Antonio;*
Except 'tis Jealousie: Yet how can that be?
If *Cælia's* vitious there's no vertuous Women.
But now I think how much he rail'd at Marriage,
And more our Arguments concerning doubt,
These things perswade he's Jealous! But of whom?
The more I think, the more I am confounded!
How Clouded Man
Doubts first, and from one doubt doth soon proceed
A thousand more in solving of the first;
Like Nighted Travellers we lose our way;
Then every *Ignis Fatuus* makes us stray.
By the false Lights of Reason led about,
Till we arrive where we at first set out:
"Nor shall we e're Truths perfect High-way see,
Till dawns the Day-break of Eternity."

[Exit.

37 Enter Eugenia.

Eug. I am amaz'd the Nurse should stay so long;
My Anger makes each minute seem an hour:
That Woman is a thing made up of mischief;
Some Fatal Devil sure did guide the Choyce
My Mother made, in choosing her our Nurse.
She's Fool to th' height: And yet hath wit enough
To tread all Labyrinths of Treachery;
But that's no wonder: For who's Treacherous
That wants not Eyes to see it's ugly Form?
For now I fear, and I believe not vainly,
That Villain, *Jasper,* knows all my concerns,
Or what could prompt him to that Impudence
He did express in his address today.

Enter Nurse.

Thou fatal Hagg, thou Mother of all mischief,
What Devil taught thy perjur'd Tongue the way
To tell the shame which thou didst first occasion?

Nurse. Pray what ayls you, Madam, are you mad?

Eug. I wish I was, as I have cause enough,
For then I should not know the shame attends me,
In being Table-talk for every Rascal,
As thou (Hell thank thee for it) now hast made me.

Nurse. I made you Table-talk! There's no such thing;
I've been too faithful to you, that I have;
Losing my sleep full oft to watch your pleasure.
And is this all I get? It is no matter, I
Shall be even with you.

Eug. Threaten on (for thou hast Acted all thy threats, Imp)
In letting *Jasper* know my shame and folly.

Nurse. Jasper knows nothing, that he does not, from me,
And I will ask him; fore your face, I will,
If I e're said *Francisco* lay with you.

Eug. 'Tis plain, thy guilt transported thee to madness,
Else thou wouldst never make thy Tongue a Herauld
So loud, for to proclaim to all the House
The Action you'd perswade me still is secret.

38*Nurse.* If you talk lowd your self, why may not I?
But I'le bring *Jasper* to you shall deny all.

Eug. What mischief upon mischief she designs?
Dost think, like thine, my Modesty is gone?
To have this argu'd out before my face
And such a Villaine by?—

*Nurse.*A Villain, say you?
No Villain neither, I wou'd have you know;
No more then is *Francisco*: pick that bone,
Or if you will, I'le bid *Gerardo* do it.
Dee' think to rail at me? Is that my thanks?

Eug. My feares I see will force me to dissemble;
Nurse, I but try'd thy patience; I believe
Thou would'st not tell that secret for the world,
No, tho' it were to *Jasper*.

Nurse. Jasper's an honest fellow, and no Villain;
And did he know a secret, he could keep it.

Eug. But have you told it then?

Nurse. No matter what I've done, I will not tell you,
Because you vext and rated at me so.

Eug. Well, Nurse, I did believe you lov'd me better.

[Weeps.

And wou'd trust me with any thing you did,
But I perceive your kindness all for *Jasper*.

Nurse. I love *Jasper* well, and love you too,
And you shall have no wrong I warrant you.

Eug. The thing is plain, I need not ask no further.
But where's the remedy? Nurse, prethee tell me,
What did *Francisco* say unto my message?

Nurse. I, there's a bus'ness now worth asking for.
He sayes, he's glad you'l condescend to meet;
Nay, he's a glad man, I'le tell you that, i' faith,
He bid me say, you were a gallant Girle,
So to Revenge his quarrel on *Gerardo*.

Eug. Gerardo, said you! O thy mouth's a Sieve!
There's not a secret thou canst keep a moment;
Did I not charge thee not to name *Gerardo,*
Till I should speak of it myself to him?
39 Nay, 'tis the greatest motive makes me meet him,
For to prevent the mischiefs else may follow;
Well, I am curst for sin, and thou art made
The cause o' th' sin, and curse that does attend it.

Nur. What, are you got to railing again for nothing?
Pray who has most discretion to tell a bus'ness,
You, or I? But you, forsooth, are grown so proud of late
Because you hope to Marry *Don Gerardo;*
That there's no speaking to you: Marry gip.
'Faith I shall spoil your Market.

[Exit.

*Eug.*Do thy worst
(for I am resolv'd to suffer once for all)
Death would be better then this Slavery,
And that's the worst can happen
Should she tell my Brother, or *Gerardo*, my whole story;
That's dying once, but I by fear thus fool'd,
Do hourly dye, since still I Death behold.

[Exit.

Enter Jasper and Antonio.

Jasp. My Lord, I'm confident this is the House,
Wherein the Woman Lives I told you of.

Anto. Knock then; and if she comes, do you speak to her,
I'le stand aloof a while, and hear you talk.

[Jasper knocks.

Enter Witch with a block Rod, which she turns over her Head, whilst Jasper makes a private sign of his Lord's being there.

Jasp. Hail, Reverend Mother; I suppose you are
That famous Artist who Commands this House,
Which if you be, with confidence I beg,
You would resolve some Questions I should ask;
Which if you please to do, my gratitude
Shall be proportion'd to the kindness done.

Witch. What prating Fellow's here? Your Lord *Antonio*
Need not to doubt my Art, or if he did,
He might have sent some wiser Man to try me.
Come, come, my Lord,
I am no Cheating Chymist, that requires
A Faith in Fools to make his work successful.
No, no, my Power is boundless, I can search
The secrets of your Soul, and when I've done
Solve all the doubts that there possess your mind;
That Women should be Women, is no wonder.

Anto. But that Women should turn Devils, is.

Witch. No, no, my Lord, I am no Devil neither.

Anto. Mother! I meant not you, when I said so.

Witch. Son, Son, excuse it not, you have no cause
To love us Women much, and I'm not angry
At what you said, though I know what you meant.

Ant. Then, Mother, by these Powers you practice by,
I do Conjure you, shew me all the truth
Of what you know concerns my coming hither.

Witch. Come, enter in, my Lord, and nothing fear;
There's not a doubt of yours but shall be clear.
I've sent a Spirit out, who will e're long,
Bring all the Names of those have done you wrong.

[Ex. and return.

Enter Antonio, Jasper, *and Witch, as in the House; in the Scenes a Chair, by which* Jasper stands, and Witch goes round.

Witch. Sit in this Chair, my Lord, whilst I do draw
A Sacred Line, which shall the Spirits aw.
About, about, I tread a Round,
Where I tread is Sacred Ground.
Thus and thus the Air I charm,
To keep my Circle free from harm;
Thus I sprinkle Water pure,
And by it all the Charm secure;
The Spirits that fiery are dare not come near us,
Earth, Air, and Water do make e'm to fear us.
Then boldly sit, boldly see, boldly despise
What Spirits soever do happen to rise.

Witch sings.

Rise, arise, arise, rise and come away,
My little pretty Spirit Puncula:
What, not appear at thy Mistresses call,
I'le surely torment thee; thou shalt not suck at all.
Arise then, I say—

[Spirit within sings.

41GSpir. I come, I come away,
The Wind it blows hard, and forces me astray.

Witch. Let's wait a little, he'l appear, my Lord.

Anto. Fear seizes me so fast, that all my Spirits
Retire, and leave an Ague in my Joynts.

Enter a Spirit.

Witch. Come, have you done
What I gave you in charge,
If you have, I command you to tell it at large.

Spirit sings.
As you bid, I did go to the Caverns below
Where the Spirits Inhabit that Govern the Wind.
And though in their motions they be,
And see
Far, far quicker than we,
Yet no Intelligence there I could find.
From thence, like Lightning, I shot to the Pole,
Where at a hole
I glided to the Region of the Air:
But the Spirits above
Do Mankind so love,
That they drove me from them with despair.
From thence, in a moment, to Ætna I came,
Where the Spirits of fire that Inhabit that flame:
Told me, all that I sought for they knew;
Though to Spirits of Earth,
As I am by Birth;
They'd not tell it; yet hither they flew.
And hereabouts they stay, till you pray,
And attone them with Offerings to tell your desire;
For these from of Old
Have been Lovers of Gold,
The Mettles being Govern'd by Spirits of fire.

[Exit.

Witch. It's necessary, Son, you throw them something, for o're these Spirits I have no Command.

Anto. Oh, any thing; take this and throw it them;
But do release me of the fear I'm in,
And quickly solve my doubts, take all I have.

42*Witch.* There is Gold, there is Gold to you Spirits of fire;
He does willingly offer what you do desire.

Enter first Spirit, second Spirit Ascends. After some flashes of fire they sing.

1. Spir. What Spirit did Lewis attend?

2. Spir. It was I.

1. Spir. Declare to that Lord what you know.

2. Spir. I need not, the cause he did dye
Was that truth to him known long ago.

Chor. He's dead, he's dead, he's dead, and now
For hot desires,
In endless fires
Must Live, must now forever Live with us below.

Chor. He's dead, he's dead, &c.

Anto. Horrid and wonderful.

1. Spir. Who all Cælia's Crimes does know?

2. Spir. It is I, but must not shew
All her ill,
For I will

[Third Spirit Ascends.

Fit her better e're she go
To her Paramour below.

3. Spir. But I that Francisco attend,
Can declare,
That he as a Friend
To Don Lewis doth share

I'th' stolen Embraces of Cælia's sweet Arms;
They kiss and lye down,
Then Lewis bemoan,
Thus with thoughts of Revenge they double Loves charms.

Chor. They kiss and lye, &c.

Anto. Thus I have warm'd a Viper in my bosom,
That wanted only heat enough to sting me,
And give me Death it self.

1. Spir. After him can Pedro stay til't be day;
Thus they sport the Night away,
Flora watching whilst they do
Laugh at you,
Saying, where's the Cuckold now?

43G2

1. Spir. They sport.

2. Spir. They laugh.

3. Spir. They kiss and play,
Till your return, doth make e'm mourn,
And spoils their Holy~day.

Chor. Thus they will do untill they dye,
When we in Hell, shall think it well
To have their pleasant Company.

[They Descend.

Anto. And that shall be this Night; make ready then
Fires that may fit so brave a pack of Letchers;
If you delight in Offerings; and for Gold
Can but increase their Torments, I will sell
All my Estate to turn it into that,
Daily to add more fewel to their flames.
Let Fools that spend their Wealth on Priests for Prayers,
Be Cheated still, I'le take a surer way,
Torments for Souls are penny-worths I'le buy,
And there is Reason in it; for 'tis likely
Hell may take Bribes, when surely Heav'n won't.

Oh Excellent project! Is't not a good one, *Jasper*?
By Hell it self, this Night Hell hath e'm all.

Witch. Your Lordship's much disturb'd, I by my Art
Will cause the Air to give a Melody,
So to compose your Spirits to themselves.

[She waves her stick. Musick and an Antick Dance of Devils handing the Purse (Antonio threw) to one another, toward the Close of which a noise without makes both Musick and Dance stop: But beginning again, a noise within makes e'm flye. The Witch trembles.

Within. Break op'e the doors, nay, sure enough they're here.

Anto. By Heav'n some Cheat, for these can be no Devils.
I'le follow e'm, and see—

[Draws his Sword.

Jasp. It is some trick to draw you from the Circle.

[Jasp. holds him.

Anto. Be what it will, Death cannot make me worse;
Unhand me then, or I will sheath this in you.

[Exit.

Witch. O, we're undone, the Officers will enter,

[Noise continues.

and my Lord will see the holes they creep into,
44 and so discover them, then we shall all be hang'd.
I'le tell my Lord the truth of all the Cheat,
and that way save my Life.

Jasp. What's that? No stratagem to help it?
Have you no hole near us, Aunt?

Witch. Yes, here is one, but should we go into't,
The other taken once, will soon betray us.

Jasp. I'le hazzard that, rather then certain Death.
And therefore to save one, I'le hide you there.

[Kills her.

Witch. O thou ungrateful Dog, dost kill me for my Love?

[Runs her through often, then throws her into the hole, she shun'd him, then lyes down and trembles.*Jasp.* No muttering, Aunt, dye quietly, and lye as
quietly; 'tis the greatest kindness you can
do me; So, now a ready lye clears all I hope.

Enter Antonio.

Anto. The Officers entring, they all vanish'd.

Jasp. The last is well.

Anto. Where's the Witch? What makes you tremble so?

Jasp. O, do not take me too, good Devil, do not.

Anto. What ayls the Fellow? *Jasper*, don't you know me?

Jasp. Alas, is't you, my Lord?

Anto. Ay, where's the Witch?

Jasp. She got upon a fiery Dragons back,
And mounted like a Rocket through the Air,
Leaving me half distracted.

Anto. 'Tis strange and wonderful.

[Enter Captain and Watch.

1. Watch. Here's two of them.

Capt. My Lord *Antonio*! 'Tis strange to meet you thus
in a suspitious House so late in the Evening.

Anto. Riding by the River side to take the Air,
My Horse threw me, which made me see
For some convenient House to rest a while,
And met with this, wherein I have slept this hour,
And I believe had done so longer yet,
Had not your noise awak'd me.

Capt. My Lord, I've no Commission to enquire,
Into Persons bus'ness of your eminent Rank;
It is for other Men that I search now,

Some half a score the most notorious Rogues
About the Town were seen to enter here.
Saw you none such, my Lord?

Anto. No, on my Honour;
For since I enter'd here, no human shape
Was seen by me, but one Old wither'd Woman;
And where she's gone, I know not.

Capt. My Lord, that Woman is the greatest Cheat
About the Town; the simple think her a Witch;
But I can witness for her she is none;
My Lord, you'l pardon me, if I search for her.

Anto. With all my heart: Pray find her if you can;
'Twas my misfortune doubled to light here.

Capt. It might have prov'd so:
search the House.

[Exit Watch.

I'le tell your Lordship what I know of her.
Walking my Round one Night, who should I meet,
But (as I thought) two Devils, by their shapes;
An Old one, and a Young one, so they seem'd:
At first the sight amaz'd me, but at last
My Reason telling me, if they were Spirits,
The mischief they intended they might do,
Though I should run away: I bid my Guard
Stand, whilst my self advanc'd near these shapes,
Which as I did, the little Devil fled, th' other seem'd
To turn it's Eyes to fire, and glare upon me;
I still advanc'd, Arm'd with my former thoughts,
And as I nearer came, the fire grew duller,
Yet still it stood, for truly it could not run,
Proving, when I laid hold on't, this Old Woman,
Cas'd in a Leopard's skin; the fiery Eyes
Prov'd but two Lobster-shells: So she confessing,
That for a Living she did use these Cheats,
Helping poor People to their stolen Goods,
In Devils shapes to countenance the Trade.

And that the other was a little Boy,
Train'd up as her Familiar, whom she producing,
46 I only threaten'd them, and let them go.

Anto. A subtle Cheat it was, and very likely,
And you deserv'd Reward that did detect it.

Jasp. A Halter it should be, were I to give it.

[Aside.

Enter the Watch with one of the Devils Remarkable Habits, and a Viol.

1. Watch. We've search'd sufficiently, but all we find
Is a poor Devils skin, and a base Viol.

Capt. I, this is like the other, I'm glad 'twas found,
'Twill prove the story true I told your Lordship.

Anto. It does, to my amazement.

Capt. I'm glad it was my hap to meet you here,
Your Lordship might have got some mischief else.

Anto. I might indeed, and I'm beholding to you:
And, Captain, take my word, I'le speak your worth
To the Vice-Roy, who is my Kinsman,
And will take care for to advance your merit.

Capt. In that you'l bind my Service: Yet, my Lord,
shall I not wait your Lordship to your House?

Anto. No, 'twill be wonder'd at, besides, I've Horses here.

Capt. Then Health and a good Night attend your Lordship.

Anto. I thank you. Captain; here, Watch, there's something for you.

1. Watch. Bless your Noble Lordship.

[Ex. Capt. and Watch.

Anto. Jasper! Did you hear this?

Jasp. Ay, my good Lord, and wonder at it too;
but I do still believe she is a Witch, and only

did pretend such things to the Captain,
to save a Burning from th' Inquisition.

Anto. Fetch our Horses.

[Exit Jasper.

I do observe this Rogue
Strangely to be amaz'd, what er'es the matter;
I do believe that this was all some Cheat.
Yet how could that be too, who could Name *Lewis*.
But I am mad to be deluded thus!
For now I think on't better; in my Passion
I hinted *Lewis* as a proof for all;
47 And then this Rogue stood by—Ay, there it is—
He's a Confederate, and contriv'd all this,
To be Reveng'd, but I'le dissemble yet,
And trace his mischiefs further, then I'le kill him,
And stop his mouth from publishing my folly:
Had not this Accident so strangely happen'd,
What mischief had I done before the Morning:
I'le put him to his Tryal in the Garden;
Which if he fail in, there shall end his Life,
And he'l deserve it too, when mischiefs tend
To such a height, they must in mischief end.
He that contriv'd so many to destroy,
Will scarce be punish'd if he barely dye,
Therefore his Villany shall further swell,
When'ts at the height I'le Lanch his Soul to hell.

[Exit.

Enter Francisco and Sebastian.

Sebast. Couzen, believe me, I am loath to go.
And I could likewise wish that you were so.
Oft have I fear'd the danger when I went,
Yet dreaded more the sin then punishment.
For I consider'd, should I then be slain,
That Death would but begin an endless pain;
Then pardon me, though I could well obey
All Friendships Laws, I dare not do't this way.

Fran. Sure Couzen, you are sick, or lately have
Had melancholy thoughts about a Grave:
Is this *Sebastian*, he, whose ready hand
Was quick to Act all Friendship did Command?
He, who no sooner heard *Francisco* say,
A Danger's there, but made that strait his way,
And now he's turn'd my Ghostly Father sure.

Sebast. I would, so I might make a Ghostly Cure.
Francisco, thou art sick, and so am I;
Sick at our Souls, and shou'd we chance to dye
E're our Disease was Cur'd, 'tis ten to one,
We should in an Eternal Feaver groan.

48*Fran.* Come, prethee say no more, 'tis ominous,
I wonder much what 'tis shou'd make thee thus.
Come, you must go this Night: I'le tell you why,
'Twill be the last, for she's to Marry,
To Marry *Don Gerardo*! O 'tis rare,
I am Reveng'd to th' purpose.

*Sebast.*Sure you are
Turn'd Coward, or you ne're wou'd glory in
Revenge so base, this doubles all your sin.
Gerardo's brave, and sure all Honour bleeds,
When such are Wounded by Ignoble deeds.
It is the Curse of Man, that he must be
Subject to shame by Womens Levity;
But hold, I wrong *Eugenia,* if I blame
Her, and not you alone, for all her shame.
You Rob'd her of her Chastity by force,
Though fear of shame still kept her from Remorse.

Fran. Pish! Force! That was her policy to you,
She did no more then what all Women do,
Seem to resist what they do most desire,
To raise the flame, yet seem to cool the fire;
Believe this Truth, *Sebastian*, Women can
Resist it, and perform it more then Man.

Sebast. Thus like the Devils we at first betray
Their Innocence, then blame on them we lay;
As if their guilt cou'd have another cause
Then that which it from our Temptation draws.

Fran. Let it be so, I'le not dispute it now;
It grows too near the time that I should go,
And though my Actions do so much offend,
I will not doubt to find another Friend.

Sebast. Do you so little prize *Eugenia's* Fame,
That you can suffer more to know her shame?

Fran. Sebastian, you mistake, I do not go
This Night on the same terms I us'd to do.
No, 'tis to take my leave, for she does vow
In spight of fear she is turn'd vertuous now.

49H*Sebast.* Nay, then I'le go my self, happen what will,
For it is only dang'rous to do ill;
My Company her Vertue may protect,
And I should sin, if that I did neglect.

Fran. That shall not need, for I'm resolv'd to speak
Nothing that may her Resolution break.

Sebast. Go boldly then, for in a cause so good
He's more then Coward fears to shed his Blood;
And though I think *Antonio* would be glad
That he our Lives at such advantage had;
Yet I this Night durst boldly meet him there,
Since in my Breast such Innocence I wear;
By this security I plainly feel
'Tis guilt that wounds us deeper far then steel.

[Exeunt.

Enter Cælia and Eugenia.

Cæl. Blame not my Husband, Sister, 'twas my fault,
I strove 'gainst Reason to oppose his Will.
Had I forborn my importunity,
'Tis ten to one he had not been so wilful;

Husband's prerogatives are absolute,
Their wills we must obey, and not dispute.

Eug. I beg his Pardon, if I think amiss,
But I believe there's some design in this;
His Eyes shew'd more of Anger then could be
A bare concern for's Friend's Infirmity.

Cæl. I will no censure on his Actions lay,
My Duty is for their success to pray.

Enter Don Gerardo.

Ger. Your Servant, Ladies, where is *Don Antonio*?

Cæl. Why, at *Don Johns*, my Lord, do not you know it?

Ger. Then he is not come back, as I had thought.

Cæl. My Lord, why thought you so?

Ger. Madam, I did not know but that he might,
Since 'tis not five hours bus'ness to Ride thither,
And to return again; but, Madam, pray
How came the Lord *Francisco* to be here?
I think he does not use it.

Eug. Francisco! O my fears!

Cæl. No sure, my Lord, he ne're came within these doors
Since my good Father dy'd.

Ger. Sure I'm mistaken, Madam, if I did not
Meet him just now as he came forth this Room:
And more, he shak'd his head in Anger at me.

Cæl. I'm sure, my Lord, you're mistaken much,
For you're the first that enter'd here but us.

Ger. It may be I'm mistaken.

Cæl. Yes, sure, my Lord, you are.

Ger. Madam, if your Commands

[To Eugenia.

Extend to any thing within my pow'r, pray name it,
I shall be proud to serve you; else I'm gone,
For I have certain bus'ness does require it.

Eug. The greatest Service you can do to me,
Is to be careful of your self, my Lord.

Ger. This kindness doth oblige me, pardon my haste,
Good Night, and Rest unto your Ladyships.

[Exit.

Cæl. Good Night, my Lord; *Flora* is so possest her Dream is true, she dare not venture in that Room again.

Eug. She is not such a Fool, sure.

Cæl. Well, Sister, I am not well, and will to Bed;
the Nurse will wait on you, I'le send her to you.
Come, *Flora*, go with me.

[Ex. Cæl. and Flora.

Eug. Madam, good Rest unto you.
This I can wish to her, whilst I must want it:
Gerardo sure has some Intelligence
Of *Don Francisco*'s coming to me;
Or else why Nam'd he him, for well he knows
He never us'd to make a Visit here:
Well, if he does, I cannot help it now.
The time draws nigh,
That I must meet *Francisco*! Oh, that word
Gives heaviness a new unto my Soul,
And makes my thoughts run backwards,
The Accidents oth' day seems Ominous
51H2 To all the House, but most of all to me,
My guilty Breast feels most of misery.
This time will quickly over, then I shall
See what they tend to, or not see at all.
"There's comfort yet, that miseries at height
Lose their worst property, which is to fright."

[Exit.

The End of the Third Act.

Act the Fourth.

Cælia on a Couch, Flora by her.

Cæl.

F*lora*, I cannot sleep, for all my thoughts
Infected with my griefs, flye up and down,
Collecting only things to keep me waking.

Flo. I'le not stir from you, Madam, all this Night.

Cæl. Flora, thy diligence deserves Reward,
And I'le not long be backward for to thank thee.
But prethee sing that Song I love so well,
That harmony, perhaps, will Charm my cares,
And give my senses Rest.

The Song.

1.

Flor. sings.
Ah, Choridon, in vain you boast,

You still do Cloris Love;

For better 'tis your heart were lost,

Then thus suspitious prove:

You then would kill me by disdain,
But dying thus you blot my Name.

52 For all will say

Cloris was false, and went astray;
Cloris was false, and did deserve her shame.

2.

For happy shepherd, well you know,

Your Fame does mine excell;

All Gen'rous Choridons do know,

But none my Tale can tell:

Cloris, though true, must lose that Name,
But Choridon will keep his Fame;

For all will say

Cloris was false, and went astray,
Cloris was false, and did deserve her shame.

3.

But Cruel Shepherd, when you hear

That I am dead indeed,

I do believe you'l shed a tear,

Though new you have decreed,

That Cloris true must lose that Name,
For Choridon to keep his Fame;

And then you'l say

Cloris was true, and ne're did stray;
Cloris was true, and I deserve her shame.

Flora. She's faln asleep, may none but happy Dreams
Possess her Fancy.

[The Scene shuts.

Enter Antonio and Jasper in the Garden.

Anto. Your confidence in this doth much amaze me.

Jasp. Sir, still I'le pawn my Life, that what I said,
Appears e're long a truth Infallible,
And your own Eyes will bear me witness of it.

Anto. Well, pitch upon a private stand for us,
That you know most convenient.

[Ex. Jasp.

Strange it is,
If this should prove a falshood after this;
I've threaten'd him with Death upon the failer,
Yet still he has persisted to affirm it,
Besides, I climb'd the Garden Wall before him,
53 And that way gave him time for his escape,
If he'd design to make it: These Circumstances
Do half perswade 'tis true. Oh, apprehension!
So terrible the consequence appears,
It makes my brain turn round, and Night seem darker.
The Moon begins to drown her self in Clouds,
Leaving a duskish horror every where,
My sickly fancy makes the Garden seem
Like those benighted Groves in *Plato's* Kingdoms,
Which Poets fancy that the damn'd inhabit.

Jasp. My Lord, my Lord.

[Enter Jasper.

Anto. What now?

Jasp. The Garden Door just opens, step this way, lest
You be seen.

[They stand close.

Enter Francisco and Sebastian.

Fran. 'Tis hardly late enough, we'l stay a little,
For I perceive no light i' th' usual Window.

Sebast. But are you confident *Antonio's* absent?

Fran. I'm told for certain that he went from home
To see *Don John Valasco*, who is sick.

Sebast. Nay, then with safety we may walk a turn,
Though I confess, do what I can, my fears
Surmount my Reason and perswades there's danger.

Fran. A hundred times I've past it in as much,
Yet then with confidence you slighted all;

Prethee forbear to urge them any more;
I'm half turn'd Coward with your fears already.

Sebast. Let's take a turn then further from the House,
And by some other talk divert our thoughts.

[Exeunt.

Anto. Jasper, I find thy Informations true,
Thus far at least; these are my Wife's kind Couzens.
Hell rid e'm from the World.

Jasp. A hundred times they had been here before
In as much danger: Mark you that, my Lord?

Anto. I, and in Soul retorted back the Lye,
For they in all their Lives ne're knew a danger
Equal to that they're near: Heark! how the Owl
54 Summons their Souls to take a flight with her,
Where they shall be Eternally benighted:
Now I again believe it was a Witch;
For here me-thinks I see a thousand Devils
Waiting in the Air with fire-forks in their hands,
Just as our City Serjeants wait with Maces,
To toss their Souls to their Eternal Prison;
Look there, that flash of Lightning does confirm it.
Nay, do but stay a little, you shall have all.
All, all; not a Soul of e'm shall escape this Night.
No, no, 'twill spoil good Company to part them,
But hold, a Light appears, draw back to cover.

[Exeunt.

Enter Francisco and Sebastian.

Sebast. The Light is there, make haste and give the sign.

Francisco strikes a Key upon his Sword; Eugenia appears above in Cælia's Gown.

Eug. Who's there, *Francisco*?

Fran. The same, and would desire your Company below.

Eug. This distance fits us better! Oh, *Francisco,*
Had we but alwayes kept it, I had been
A spotless Off'ring to my Bridal Bed,
But now must cloud my Marriage Joys with shame,
And fear of what will follow.

Fran. Pray descend, this distance is not safe,
The Family may chance o're hear our words.

Eug. I've more cause, should I come down,
You would attempt my strength, and Argument
To violate my Vows, as first you did
My Virgin-Honour.

Fran. No, upon my Life, do but descend,
And may the Heav'ns pour all their Vengeance on me
If I do attempt you with a sillable
To break your Resolution.

Eug. Is any with you?

Fran. Yes, my Friend, *Sebastian*.

Eug. Let him speak, then.

Sebast. Madam, upon my Life, I will secure you,
And glory I have so much cause to do it.

She takes the Light from above.*Eug.* Your Virtue I rely on for my safety.

Enter Antonio and Jasper.

Anto. I cannot hear their words, yet I'm sure
It's *Cælia's* there, her Habit tells me that.
Let's draw a little nearer.

Sebast. Look there, *Francisco,* are not those two Men
Are creeping there?

Fran.'Tis so, let's slip aside.

[Ex. Fran. and Sebastian.

Enter Eugenia below.

Eug. Where are you, Couzen *Francisco*? Are you there?

Anto. I, here, here, perfidious Woman.

[Stabs her, she falls.

Eug. Oh, *Francisco,* 'tis an inhuman deed,

[Ex. Ant., Jasp.

To kill me thus, 'cause I would sin no longer,
But thou hast kept thy word, and took thy leave.
As I must now, of all the World, and thee—oh, oh—

Enter Gerardo and Servant.

Ger. Pray Heav'n I be'n't too late, the Garden door
So open makes me wonder: Heard you no groans?

Serv. I think I did, my Lord; heark, Sir again.

Eug. Oh, oh; I fain would live a little longer,
If but to ask forgiveness of *Gerardo,*
My Soul will scarce reach Heav'n without his Pardon.

Ger. Who's that wou'd go to Heav'n, and wants my Pardon?
Take it, what e're thou art, and mayst thou be
Happy in Death, what e're thou didst design.

Eug. Is that *Gerardo's* Voyce? Sure loss of Blood
Doth make my fancy Idle: Is't *Gerardo*?

Ger. Thou greatest Blessing of my Soul, it is.

Eug. No, no, my Lord, you will abhor my Name,
When I shall tell the story made me thus.

Ger. Heav'n knows I sooner should abhor my Life:
But tell me the Author of this horrid mischief,
That I may flye as quick to my Revenge,
As these sad thoughts do seize upon thy Soul.

Eug. When you shall hear my story, your Revenge
56 Will, as I fear, vent against me in Curses.

Ger. Were thy Crimes great as theirs that left thee thus
By all thy Virgin hopes I would not Curse thee.

Eug. My Lord, that's it you are deceiv'd in.

Ger. Nay, now thou rav'st—help me to bend her body
Her loss of Blood will keep her story from me;
And I shall Live i'th' dark, and ne're Revenge her.

Eug. Alas, my Lord, my Couzen, base *Francisco,*
Being let in by my accursed Nurse,
Came to my bed, and there by force and strength obtain'd
His hated ends.

Ger. Oh, damn'd Villain, he shall not long survive
To boast of it.

Eug. Had I staid there, and not consented further,
I should have needed pity, and not pardon.

Ger. Tell all the rest, for this is so surprizing,
I'd fain perswade my self it was a Dream.

Eug. After this Fatal loss, a shame succeeded,
Shame that produc'd fear; infus'd by threats
Urg'd both by him and her, wherein they said,
If I refus'd to grant that willingly,
Which he at first did force, they would declare
The Action to the World, so to disgrace me.

Ger. O that old wrinkl'd Hag! that she should plot this.

Eug. What will not wicked Age effect for Gold?
But they at last made fear or'e-come my Vertue,
And I by that made all their guilt my own,
Meeting him here still when he did appoint.

Ger. Well, this confest, how came you by these Wounds?

Eug. My Lord, *Francisco* did entreat my Company
This Night; when as I enter'd,
Without a word, but here, perfidious Woman,
He stab'd me in the Breast, and left me thus.

Ger. Hadst thou been dead, and Angels told the story,
I should have thought, in Envy of thy worth,
They had invented it, and ne're believ'd it.

Eug. I have no breath to tell you; oh, my Lord,
57I I do forget, they still are in the Garden—
Have a care of—

[Dyes.

Ger. Have a care of what? Oh, speak, *Eugenia*, speak.
She's gone, she's gone; and could not tell her mind:
What is't I must have a care on! O some Angel
That waits to shew her Soul the way to Heav'n,
Come back and tell me, what it was she meant:
Was it her Reputation she took care of?
No, no, that cannot be, had it been that,
She might have kept the story to her self:
And then been Canoniz'd: Was it of me
She did express her care? If so, 'twas needless;
For he that lets me Live to kill *Francisco,*
Though he does so by me, when that is done,
Shall have my thanks and Prayers i'th' other World;
But stay, they're in the Garden, I'le go look e'm,
"For if Revenge so just I do delay,
I shall deserve Heav'ns Vengeance for the stay."

[Exeunt.

Enter Francisco and Sebastian.

Fran. Who should they be I wonder talk'd so long?

Sebast. Sure, when she found us not, she would retire.

Fran. No doubt on't; yet I am not satisfy'd what two
Those were, and why they staid so long.
Could your Ear reach to understand their words?

Sebast. No, not a syllable more then a humming noise.

Fran. Nor mine; but now they're gone, let's walk that way,
'Twill be the best to miss them.

Sebast. Content.

[Exeunt.

Enter Don Gerardo and Servant.

Ger. It is in vain to look e'm if they hide,
The Garden's large; besides perhaps they're gone;
We'l to the Body.

*Serv.*You're by it now, my Lord.

Ger. This Accident amazes me so much,
I go I know not where.

58 Enter Francisco and Sebastian.

Serv. See there, my Lord, two Men.

Fran. W'are pretty near the Window, there's no Light.

Ger. Have at thy heart, *Francisco,*
This Token from *Eugenia.*

[Ger. and servant draw.

*Fran.*They Fight, the Servant shoots Sebastian just as Francisco runs Gerardo through, which pursuing, Servant kills him too. Nay, then, at thine: Be whom thou wilt, that Name
Tells me thou'rt no Friend.

Sebast. Courage, *Sebastian's* by thee.
My fears are come about, for I am kill'd;
Francisco, fare thee well.

[Dyes.]

Fran. 'Tis double Death to see my Friend dye thus.
Was't not enough, you Fates, to take my Life,
But I must guilty be of murd'ring him.

Serv. My Lord, how do you?

Ger. Making what haste I can to meet *Eugenia.*

Serv. O me! Unfortunate!

Ger. Bewail me not; Death is a pleasure to me,
Since I can see *Francisco* lye there by me;
But ask him e're I dye,
What made him kill *Eugenia*?

Fran. What, is *Eugenia* Dead?

Ger. Why seems it strange to thee, who basely hast
First Rob'd her of her Honour, then of Life.

Fran. Gerardo, it was cruelty to kill her, being as
Yet she had not done thee wrong, and dying,
I rejoyce I have Reveng'd her.

Ger. Francisco, sure thy Crimes have made thee Devil,
Or thou would'st ne're transfer thy Treachery
By murd'ring her, and place it thus on me.

Fran. May I reach Heav'n as I'm Innocent
Of any Death but yours: Which if a guilt
Forgive me Heav'n and you as—

[Dyes.

Serv. He's dead, my Lord.

Ger. With such a Lye in's mouth;
O Heavenly Angels lead me not his way,
For he must alwayes walk i'th' paths of falshood;
Remove me nearer to *Eugenia's* Body;
59I2 My Spirits faint apace, and I must follow:
One word, and then farewell;
I have no time for to Reward thy care:
Here, take this Ring, and give it to my Brother,
He left it with me when he went to Travel;
Tell him I still preserv'd it for his sake,
A faithful pledge of our United Friendship.
Bid him, that by this Token he believes
Three words I left within my Cabinet
Concerning thee this Evening: He will do it,
And use thee as a Friend, as I have done.

Serv. I'le bear the Ring, but not the Message, Sir;
I ne're will seek for Friends when you are gone.

Ger. I do conjure thee do it: Tell our story too
As true as is thy self: But have a care,
Wound not *Eugenia*'s Fame more then must needs.
Francisco's and *Eugenia's* dying words
Will make it strangely dark, as 'tis to me,

But I must leave it so!
Give me thy hand, commend me to *Antonio*;
Alas! I had forgot him, pray Heav'n his story
Produce no further mischief; tell *Cælia* nothing
Befor't be day: Bus'ness comes thronging on me,
But I faint— —make but one Grave, and lay us
In it thus— —Farewell.

[Dyes.

Serv. Now dyes the justest Man the Earth contains,
And I would do so too, but that I know
Self-murderers ne're must keep him Company;
I'le set the Bodies up against the Wall,
And call the Watch; what if they say I'm guilty,
And make my Life to answer all these Deaths:
Why, let e'm do't, for Death would now be well
Since to survive his loss to me's a Hell.

[Exit.

Enter Antonio and Jasper.

Jasp. Come, come, my Lord, the coast is quiet now.

Anto. I hope that Pistol sav'd our swords a labour.

Jasp. I'm sure they could not leave the Garden yet,
But we must needs have seen e'm.

Anto. Nay, I'm sure they did not pass the Garden door,
For if they had, we should have stopt their Journey.

Jasp. I think I heard a talking up this way,
After the Pistol made us leave our Post.

Anto. Though I did leave the Door, yet still my Eye
Was bent that way, and I saw none to pass.
But stay, where's *Cælia's* Body?

Jasp. See, my Lord,
There is a Man doth hold her in his Arms.

Anto. It is *Francisco* sure! Have at his heart.

[Runs at Gerardo.

How's this, not stir! Nay, then he's dead
Already—the Moon deceives me, or it is *Gerardo*.
Oh Heav'n's! It is my Friend, dead, dead, and stiff,
And my accursed hand hath Wounded him.
This is not *Cælia* neither, but *Eugenia* in her Gown!
What strange mistakes are these?

Jasp. But who are here?

Anto. What, more!
By Heav'ns *Francisco* and his Friend *Sebastian*!
Both dead too! Death has had a Feast to Night.
Do not we Dream? As for this Womans Death,
Surely her Fathers Soul did guide my hand
To strike the blow, since needs she must betray
Her Honour to *Francisco*, in these meetings!
But oh, my Sword hath pierc'd my Friend *Gerardo*.
What Fatal Accident mixt his Blood with theirs.
But stay, there's Light appears, slip into the Grotto.

[Exeunt.

Enter Servant, Captain, and Watch, with two Torches.

Serv. Here is the dismal place I told you of,
And here the Bodies.

Capt. A fight most terrible in time of Peace!
But did *Francisco* still deny her Death?

Serv. To his last moment;
He did confess he had abus'd her,
But would have plac'd her Death upon my Lord.
61 And seem'd as much to wonder we deny'd it
As we that he did so.

Capt.What said *Sebastian*?

Serv. He scarce did speak a word after I shot him.

Capt. Had we not best to knock, and call *Antonio*?

Serv. He's not at Home.

*Capt.*Yes, but I'm sure he is.

Serv. He was not late at Night, for I was there.

Capt. That's strange, for just at shutting in o'th' Evening
I met him at a House that stands i'th' Suburbs,
Saying, he would go Home.
I think however we had best to knock.

Serv. My dying Lord made it his last desire,
That *Cælia* might not be disturb'd this Night.

Capt. Well, take the Bodies up, and keep e'm safe,
You shall to the Vice-Roy's presently with me,
I scarce perform my trust, if I detain
The knowledge of so strange an Accident
A moment from his Ears, whose Wisdom will
Direct in this, which far exceeds my skill.

[Exeunt.

Enter Antonio and Jasper.

Jasp. You see, my Lord, that I was in the right,
I only said, it was my Ladies Gown,
But never did affirm it was her Person.

Anto. And I am glad it is not: Now, if Nurse
Fails too in her discovery, I am safe,
For if we keep our Councel, all these Deaths
Lye pat amongst themselves, and there's not one,
Except *Gerardo*, that I'd wish alive;
He was my friend, and it looks Ominous,
That I should Wound him so, though after Death:
Jasper, thy diligence shan't want Reward,
But that must follow: Come, let's away.

[Exit.

Jasp. My Reward follows! I believe it does;
'Faith, my good Lord, be sure it be a good one,
Or be content to hang for Company;
62 Now hap what will, I'le rid him with this murther;
Till I do make him spend's Estate to Bribe me:

"I was his Slave before for fear; but now
I'le make him mine, since I this secret know."

[Exit.

The End of the Fourth Act.

Act the Fifth.

Cælia Discover'd in Bed, Flora by her.

Cæl.

SUre 'twas a real Pistol-shot that wak'd me,
Yet from a Dream so terrible, it did it,
That I had rather never sleep again,
Then hazzard such another. I thought I saw
Lye dead by me,
My Lord *Antonio, Don Gerardo, Jasper,*
The Nurse, *Francisco,* and the Young *Sebastian,*
With *Pedro,* and thy self; this dreadful sight,
Or else the Pistols noise, I spoke of, wak'd me,
And made me cry help, help, which frighted thee.

Flor. Why truly, Madam, it was a dreadful Dream,
And I as much was frighted at your call,
Yet, for my own part, I did hear no Pistol.

Cæl. It may be then, it only was my fancy,
For truly all my Dream seems still to me
So like a truth, that I can scarce distinguish
Whether I then did wake, or now am sleeping;
And but I see these things, and thee so plain,
I should conclude my Dream did still continue.

Flor. Pray Heav'n divert all mischief from the house,
For I have heard it said by Learned Men,
63 Nay, and Religious too, that Dreams like these.
That stick so fast upon our fancies waking,
Are guided by a power that's more then Chance,
And alwayes are portents of something like them:

I'm sure, for my own part, do what I can,
That Dream I had will not yet leave my head,
Which makes me think *Jasper* designs me mischief.

Cæl. Flora, you go too far, Dreams are but shadows
Reflected from some Acts the day preceeding,
As ours are now; for from those Accidents
Of my Lords taking *Jasper*, the Dream you told,
And *Don Gerardo's* naming of *Francisco*,
Mine now is formed: Thus they but succeed
Things past, and not prognostick things to come.

Flor. Pray Heav'ns these do not do't, but I'm afraid.

Enter Nurse, frighted with Eugenia's Ghost.

Nurse. Stand off, stand off, what makes you follow me?
I'm sure I did not kill you, if you're dead,
Or if you be not, why are you so pale? –
So, so – she's gone – but what made me come hither.

Cæl. What, do you study wayes to fright me, Nurse?
It is no proper time to play your tricks.
What makes you up at such a time of Night?
Look, how she stands amaz'd, and doth not answer;
Think you I take a pleasure to be frighted?
That you persist in't still?

Flor. What, is the Woman mad, or would be thought so?
What makes you stand and stare thus?

Nurse. Did you see no Body?

Cæl. Who should we see but an Old doting fool,
That turn'd a Child again, would Act like one,
And can't find a proper time for't neither.

Flor. What make you up so late, Nurse?

Nurse. What's that to you? It may be I sat up
To make my Lady merry with this Jest,
But now, forsooth, I'm grown too Old to please her.
You are her favourite – what, come again?
64 O, do not stare so at me!

[Shreeks.][Exit.

Cæl. There's something more in this then barely play!
How the Old Woman star'd? sure she's run mad!
For shame, or sorrow *Jasper* goes away.
Prethee follow her.

Flor. Since you will have me, Madam, I will do't,
Though I dare scarcely venture.

[Exit.

Cæl. The greatest Object pity hath, is Age,
When it returns to Childishness again,
As this Old Woman doth; and though we say,
That Age is Honourable, we only mean,
When Gravity and Wisdom are its marks,
And not gray hairs, and froward peevishness,
As ten for one, are known by to be Old,
And though we see this true, yet we would all
Prolong our time to that decrepid state,
When nothing but contempt can wait upon us;
How strangely sin dastards our very Reason,
Making that guide us to desire known ills
Rather then Joys, that promis'd we deserve not;
For the best Men through sense of guilt do fear
To change for unseen Joys their troubles here.

[Exit.

Enter Nurse.

Nurse. If this Ghost follow still, 'twill make me mad;
For sure it is a Ghost it looks so pale;
Ay, and *Eugenia's* Ghost, I'm sure it is;
But who should kill her? May be *Don Francisco*!
Oh, there it is again—It's not my fault—
Oh, do not follow me then: What shall I do?
See there again, she points unto her Breasts—
It's gone again, I fear 'twill make me mad—
I'le go to Prayers: But I forget my bus'ness,

My Lord will come, and I must let him in,
And shew him what I promis'd, or he'l kill me.

Enter Flora.

What, come again! Oh, Heav'ns! I'le stop my Eyes,

Flor. Nurse, are you mad?

Nurse. No, you would make me so! But I defie thee—
Be gone, thou Spirit, i'th' name of Heav'n, be gone.

Flor. Who should be gone?

Nurse. Thou! for thou'rt the Devil. Come not near me.

Flor. My Lady sent me to you—

Nurse. No, no, she did not, for she lov'd me always,
And would not send the Devil thus to fright me.

Flor. I am no Devil, Nurse, look upon me, I'm *Flora.*

Nurse. Ay, where's the Spirit then I saw just now?

Flor. There was no worser Spirit then my self.

Nurse. No; pray Minx, what makes you follow me?
I'le set you back again i'th' Devils Name,
Come you to spy my Actions.

Flor. No, Nurse, my Lady sent me, don't be angry,
She was afraid that you were running mad.

Nurse. I, mad, it may be so; now I am Old
I must be mad, forsooth; but time has been,
There's ne're a Servant durst have laught at me,
Nor I'le not take it now, no that I won't,
She runs after Flora, who still is too quick for her. I'le tear your Eyes out first.

Flor. Nay, softly, Nurse; so, so; ay, there!

Nurse. Where where? I see it now, It's strangely pale!
O, do not fright me so; it's gone again.
And now I shall have time to follow you;

As Flora runs away, she falls, Nurse gets upon her. Nay, now I'le tear thy Eyes out.

Flor. Oh, Nurse, Nurse! have mercy on me,
Do not scratch me so.

Nurse. I'le be thy Death, there's nothing shall preserve you.
Ah — — are you there again! The Devil, the Devil.

[Exit.

Flor. 'Twas well for me her madness work't again,
And made her take a whim to run away,
She would have kill'd me else, do what I could;
I'le stay no longer, lest she come again.
I'd not be in her fingers as I was
For all I'm worth.

[Exit.

66 Enter Captain, Watch, and Servant.

Capt. When I consider every Circumstance
Of what you tell, and what I know my self,
I must conclude, I ought not to defer
To search *Antonio*'s House: if he's from home,
As you pretend he is; It makes me think
There is some strange Intrigue design'd by him.
For why should he turn back, as you relate,
And then obscure himself in such a House?
Besides, he told me, he was strait for Home,
And yet it seems was not, as you say.

Serv. It's truth, upon my Life, he was not there
At past the hour of Nine.

Enter the little Devil, and runs and skulkes.*Watch.* Who comes there!
Captain, the Devil, the Devil!
See where he stands?

Capt. O' my Conscience! The Witches little Familiar again!
If you're afraid, let me come, I'm us'd to
It sputters like a Cat, Captain to him. These sort of Devils! Come, come, uncase,

Uncase, young Gamester, what slippery pranck
Are you about now? Don't you remember your
Last escape, Sirrah?

Devil. Pray Master don't whip me, I'le tell all.

Capt. Out with it then; where's the Old Witch, your Mistress?

Devil. Alas, Captain, she was kill'd to Night when you brought in the Watch to search our House.

Capt. Kill'd, by whom?

Devil. I know not that, but we were putting a cheat upon a Lord there, by contrivance of his Man, and when you knockt, we ran to our lurking holes to hide us, but when the Coast was clear, we came out, and seeking for my Mistress, found her dead in one of the holes thrust through her Body with a Dagger in three places.

Capt. What cheat was that you put upon the Lord?

Dev. We Acted like Devils, and in a Song made him believe his Wife did Cuckold him.

67K2*Capt.* This was *Antonio*, whom I met there, Sir.

Devil. Ay, that's his Name, a mighty furious Man,
He said, he'd kill e'm all before 'twas day.
He made me quake to hear him; I hope now,
Captain, you will let me go.

Capt. No, no, you Rogue! If he has done more mischief
You shall be hang'd, except you find your Fellows
That joyn'd i'th' cheat with you to make him Jealous.

Devil. I'le bring you presently to them, and shew you all their holes; they did but send me out to watch when the Coast was clear!

Capt. Who, say you, set you on to this design?

Devil. An ill-look'd Rogue, his Man, the Witches Nephew;
I think they call him *Jasper*.

Capt. Well, take the Boy, and call some of your Fellows,
And there surprize them all. I'le not defer
My searching to prevent the mischief
That *Don Antonio* further may design,
For I believe he had a hand in this
Was done i'th' Garden, however the mistake
Did happen to begin between the Dead.

Serv. Come, Sir, make haste, for I begin to fear
Some Tragedy is Acted in the House,
For *Don Antonio*'s Rage is alwayes quick,
And they have toucht the string will stretch it highest.

Capt. Come then, let's hasten back.

[Whistling behind the Stage.

Enter Nurse.

Nurse. Ay, that's his whistle, and I must obey't.
Why *Pedro, Pedro*! What, are you dead asleep? *Pedro,* I say.

Pedro within. Who calls?

Nurse. Pedro, rise quickly, my Lady *Cælia* wants you.

Ped. What can she want me for at such a time?

Nurse. I know not, but *Flora* came, and said you must come quickly, I think, to Ride to my Lord.

68*Ped.* I come, but I'le have a care of your tricks, Nurse.

Enter Pedro in a Night-Gown, with his sword in's hand.*Nurse.* What tricks? What do you do with your Sword?

Ped. Why, Nurse, you may have malice, and malice may seek mischief, which because you are no Witch, and cannot come through a Key-hole to compass, for ought I know, you call me out to do it—ha! What whistle's that?

[Whistle.

Nurse. What whistle! Are you mad! Go to my Lady.

Ped. Still I suspect you.

[Exeunt.

Enter Nurse, with Antonio and Jasper.

Anto. Are they together, Nurse?

Nurse. Yes, my Lord, the more's my sorrow!

Anto. Nay then, I see the Devils did speak truth;
Francisco, their kind Couzen, Whor'd them both,
By Heav'ns they took their turns, I see it plain!
O that I could invent some horrid Death,
And had but time to execute it on them;
But since I cannot, plain stabbing will do well,
The less they've here, the more they'l find in Hell.

Nurse. I hope you will not kill your Lady, Sir!

Anto. Not kill her! But I must.

Nurse. What have I done? Oh, oh.

[Cryes out oh, oh.

Anto. Hold, stop your mouth, I'le stop it for you else;
They'l hear her, and escape!
Come, *Jasper*, are you ready?

Jasp. Yes, my Lord, I follow.

[Exeunt.

Nurse. What have I done, one Murder on another?
I see 'twas he that kill'd *Eugenia* now,
By's naming *Don Francisco*; oh, that *Jasper*—
Oh, the Ghost again—what shall I do?

[Exit.

Cælia in Bed, and Flora all Bloody.

Cæl. I'm sorry that I sent thee, since she's mad,
But would 'twas day, that I might get her lookt to.

Flor. I'm sure she has scratch't my face sufficiently.

Cæl. 'Tis well it was no worse.

[Pedro knocks.

Flor. Alas! she'l come again!

69*Ped. Flora, Flora.*

[He knocks.

Flor. Who's that, *Pedro*! What's the matter with you?

Ped. Nurse call'd, and said my Lady would speak with me.

Cæl. Bid him come in.

Flor. My Lady bids you enter.

[Enter Pedro.

Cæl. Pedro, the Nurse is mad, I did not call you,
You see how she has scratcht poor *Flora*'s Face,
She came just now shreeking and staring hither;
If you could lock her up into some Room,
A noise, Exiturus, he fights, and Enters with Antonio, whom when he sees, he lets fall his point, and is kill'd. Jasper runs Flora through.
It would do well.

Ped. I hear her coming up.
Thieves, Madam, Thieves!
Oh Heav'ns, it is my Lord!

Anto. Damn'd Letcher, so it is!
What, does your Courage fail you—
There, take that—

[Runs him through.

And boast in Hell that *Don Antonio*'s Sword
Did thee the Honour to send thee thither.

Flor. O Heav'ns! My fears were true, the Rogue has kill'd me.

[Falls & dyes.

Anto. Now Monster of thy Sex, see this, and tell me
What are the effects you do expect from it?

Cæl. Death, that's less terrible then is your Anger,
Which I perceive by it's effects already,
Upon that Innocent Man cannot stay there.

Anto. Are your concerns for him, when they should be
Employ'd to Heav'n for mercy to your Soul?
Nay, then Hell take it's Quarry; this for *Don Lewis*,
This for *Don Francisco*; and take this last
For thy insatiate Lust with that damn'd Hind.

Cæl. This killing me, my Lord, is very cruel;
Since I ne're sinn'd in thought against your Honour.
This, as I do expect Eternal Rest,
Is such a Truth, that I can dye in it.

Anto. O Hell and Furies! This Womans impudence exceeds you all.
See there a Dog just wreeking from thy Bed,
Hot with the Labour you have put him to:
And yet in thought you did not wrong my Honour.

Cæl. From my Bed, my Lord! You are abus'd;
That fellow was not here full half a minute,
E're your self enter'd! Oh, I can no more—
Heav'n and the World grant Pardon for my Blood.
For truth it self bears witness; I dare say
That more I sorrow for your guilt then Death.

Anto. If this be true, tell me as thou art dying,
What made him here at such a time o' Night?

Cæl. I cannot tell more, then that the Nurse did send him;
And she's run mad with guilt, or shame, or both!
Oh, I can say no more—the Room turns Round;
My Lord, farewell—Heav'n pardon you all Blood,
As I forgive you mine—oh, oh—

[Dyes.

Anto. Her Death both staggers, and amazes me!
Are these Dead too?

*Ped.*Not yet, my Lord, I am not.
Your Sword hath left me some small time for Prayers,

And it had need; for I believe few Souls
Can be assur'd to find their way to heav'n
Without more warning to begin their Journey.
But yet I do not find much cause for doubt.

Anto. Nay, if thou'st hopes, by that I do conjure thee
Tell me, what brought thee hither?

*Ped.*The Nurses madness;
She call'd me from my Bed, and told me, *Flora*
Was sent to bid me come unto my Lady,
Which though I scarce believ'd, yet I did do't.

Anto. Why did you say it was her madness did it?

Ped. My Lady said she was so, for she came
Not long before shreeking into this Chamber,
So as you enter'd I was going down
To lock her up till morning in some Room:
This, as I hope for heav'n, my Lord, is true.

Anto. Then 'tis as true, that I must never hope for it,
For I have kill'd a Wife of such obedience—
But hold, I'le pump the Nurse—who set her on
To tell me this.

[Enter Nurse frighted.

71*Nurse.* O! whether will you drive me!
Be gone, be gone!

Anto. Here, here she comes, I'le make her tell me all.

Jasper Runs Nurse through but is staid by Antonio.*Jasp.* But I'le prevent the story if I can.—

Anto. What, does the Villain mean to kill her yet?

Jasp. Does she not deserve it? To invent such lyes,
And do such mischiefs with them.

Nurse. O thou damn'd Rogue! 'Twas thou that made me do't.

Jasp. You lying Witch, be damn'd—

[Offers at her again.

Anto. Forbear, you Rogue, I'le do as much for you else.
Speak, why you did it?

Nurse. My Lord, he threaten'd me, and made me do't;
And taught me to call *Pedro* when you knockt.

Jasper runs Anto. behind.*Ped.* Look to your self, my Lord, he'l kill you else.

Jasp. This way is only left—hell take your Tongue.

Anto. Ah, thou hast kill'd me; yet I have strength enough
They fight. A noise without. Jasper is mortally wounded. To send thy Soul to hell.

Jasp. 'Tis done, I am catch'd at last in my
own Trap. Oh, I deserve my Death for want
of fore-sight, to let him Live a spye upon my Actions.
Runs Pedro through as he lyes, and Nurse. I should have serv'd you thus, and thus,
and thus—and you too thus.

Ped. Oh, O, O!

[Pedro and Nurse Dye.

Anto. Infernal Monster! how his malice lasts.

Within. This way's the noise.

Enter Captain, Watch, and Servant.

Capt. What horrid sight is this? We come too late.

Anto. Too late indeed, except you'd come to save
The best of Wives that there lyes murder'd
By my accursed hand.

Capt. What, *Cælia* dead too! What made you do't, my Lord?

Jasp. Alas! he cannot tell; the Jealous fool
Was but an Instrument in my Revenge;
'Tis only I can tell you why she dy'd.
But yet I would not give that satisfaction,
Did I not fear my Name would be forgotten,

Except this Tale of my Revenge was known;
72 In which I shall live famous. –

*Serv.*O thou Dogg!
Dost glory in the mischiefs thou hast done?

Jasp. I, and have reason; name the man that ever
Did in one Day contrive so many Murders,
And make 'em all Successful.

Capt. But what should move thee to this Villainy?

Jasp. For that you will not wonder.
I am *Jasper De Monsalvo,* Heir to that Estate
This Lord doth now possess.

Anto. Ah Heav'ns! some of that desperate Banditry
Did once attempt my life.

Jasp. Yes truly –

Anto. Poor *Cælia,* 'tis no wonder thy mind did boad great mischiefs from this Fellow, being Son of one did still contrive to kill me, for what the King after just forfeiture for mighty services had given my Father.

Jasp. O Revenge!
Thy sweetness takes away the taste of Death.
But you'l lose my story; which in short is this:
That Lady lov'd me not, and therefore I
Made her Lord Jealous, took him to a Witch,
And there I fool'd him finely: Till the Jade,
Who was my Aunt indeed, at your approach
Would have discover'd all; which I prevented,
And stopt her Mouth with this: Then I contriv'd
To kill *Eugenia,* knowing she would meet
Francisco in the Garden; that I did
Because she call'd me Villain, and refus'd
To let me Whore her too, as did her Couzen;
And more, I knew the simple Lord I serv'd
When he had Murder'd her, as I should make him,
Would thank my Care, and well reward it too:

Nay, I'd have him do't for his own safety,
That still the Murder might be thought *Francisco*'s;
You know the rest i'th' Garden. I taught besides
That damn'd Old Hagg, whose fear has made me thus,
73L To put this trick on *Pedro*: I bid her call him
When she should hear us whistle, then in haste,
And all undrest send him to *Cælia*'s Chamber,
Whilst we, let in, might meet him coming thence,
Thinking the Cuckold's Rage would murder all,
And never hear 'em speak; but there I fail'd,
Their dying words betray'd me, that's the worst,
Or I had liv'd to glory in their Deaths;
But this my Comfort is, he'l not survive me,
I have done his bus'ness too before I dye.

Serv. Was er'e so Impudent a Villain seen?

Capt. I'le try to stop his wounds, that so
I may keep him for Execution.

Jasp. Stand off, by Hell,
He that comes near me finds his Death with this!
Think you I'm grown so tame to dye by Law;
No, no, I'le not endure a formal Tryal,
To be upbraided with those things I think
Deserve a Trophy rather then Contempt,
Which since I know will follow, here's my Bail,
This will deliver any Man from Jayl.
Let Cowards dye by hanging; such as I
As we live bravely, thus dare bravely dye.

[Stabs himself.

Capt. He has done well; no Excutioner
Could have been found so bad as his own hand,
And Hell will give him what he wants on Earth:
And yet, my Lord, it troubles me for you,
Since my Place binds me to secure your Person,
To answer Law for all your Rage has done.

Anto. Shame almost stops my mouth; yet, Captain, know
My wound won't give me time for that misfortune;

Stay but a little, let me fix my Eyes
On what lies here, for that alone would give me
A sudden Death, had I no other hurt.
I dare not hope for Heav'n, having done
So black a Murder on such Innocence,
And yet I do believe her Charity
74 As it did dying, still doth beg that Pardon
Might from above be granted to my soul,
Which if I miss, as I have cause to fear,
Then sure I shall be turn'd into a Devil
For ever to Torment his Cursed soul
That led me to these mischiefs.
'Twould be some ease, if Heaven but granted that,
But I begin to faint! Oh, Blessed Soul
Dart forth one Beam of Light, to guide the way,
Or I shall always wander in the dark.
Night seizes me already: yet from hence
In spight of death my soul shall take her flight,
Go where I will, I thus set out a right.

[Dyes.

Serv. He's dead –

Capt. By dying so, at least he's thus far happy,
That he Escapes the Punishments of Tryal,
And the Exemplar death must have attended
Which to a man so Jealous of his Fame
As he was, would have been a Hell on Earth.
Your Duty to your Lord will keep you safe,
Yet you must to the Vice-Roy go with me
To be a Witness there of what hath happn'd,
The story else will seem Incredible.

Serv. I am ready, Sir, for all you shall Command.

Capt. Oh Jealousie, thou sickness of great souls,
To what a Rage didst thou transport this Lord?
For had his Wife been false it was not good
By Murd'ring her to drown himself in Blood;

For Lust may be Excus'd since flesh is frail,
But Murder on the Soul does guilt Entail.

The Curtain Falls.

75L2

EPILOGUE

By Mr. Harris.

A Tragedy, and not Heroick Verse,
The Comick part fit only for a Farse;
No Atheism, nor any man we know
Abus'd, no repartee, nor splendid show;
But very little Bawdy, and less wit,
The Devil's in't, crys one, is this Play hit.
Faith—may be not, and may be too it will,
For Chance sometimes exceeds all rules of skill.
As he who Rageing did his Pencil throw,
And Painted that by chance, he could not draw
For we have seen, and lately too, a Play
Cry'd down by those that cannot keep away
And when they come spight of themselves they stay.
And to our sorrow we have others known,
That for their wit have Wit it self out-done,
And yet you wits, that praise 'em seldom come.
So the Goodman, oft-times for cause unknown,
Leaves well-drest Beauteous Wife for Homely Joan.
And you that Misses keep too, I'm afraid
Do sometimes make e'm Jealous of the Maid;
So if this Play not drest by rules of Art
Should with some Trick of Nature catch the heart;
We'd give you leave to rail, and never fear,
Because we're sure you'd come to do it here.
76 Gallants you see what e're you say or do,
Plays will be writ, and we shall Act 'em too.
Some will for pleasure, some for profit write,
Some for Applause, and some will do't in spight,
Such bit by Critticks, strait run mad and bite.

This does our bu'sness; but we'd have you know,
We wish we'd none but true brisk wit to show,
We silence wish that Men might hear a Play,
And wish that Vizard Mask would keep away:
But we as well might wish we were those Kings
We sometimes Act, as hope to see these things.
Then since to rail o'th' Stage and in the Pit,
Must in this sickly Age be counted Wit;
And that th' Infection cannot be subdu'd,
We Actors for our own sakes do conclude,
The Itch to write and rail will ne're be cur'd,
And therefore faith let 'em be both Endur'd.

FINIS.

ERRATA.

The listed corrections, included in the original book, have been made and marked in the text.

PAge 17. Line 36. For *your* read *their*. p. 23. l. 19. f. *Taylors* r. *Juglers*. p. 31. l. 18. r. *my fears*. p. 38. l. 6. r. *Villain by*. p. 51. l. 6. f. *first* r. *worst*. p. 53. l. 35. f. *his* r. *in*. p. 57. l. 11. f. *there* r. *then*. p. 58. l. 36. f. *this* r. *his*.

THE AUGUSTAN REPRINT SOCIETY

ANNOUNCES ITS

Publications for the Third Year (1948-1949)

Many of the listed titles are or will be available from Project Gutenberg. Where possible, a link to the e-text is given.

At least two items will be printed from each of the *three* following groups:

Men, Manners, and Critics

Series IV:
Sir John Falstaff (pseud.), *The Theatre* (1720).
Aaron Hill, Preface to *The Creation*; and Thomas Brereton, Preface to *Esther*.
Ned Ward, Selected Tracts.

Drama

Series V:
Edward Moore, *The Gamester* (1753).
Nevil Payne, *Fatal Jealousy* (1673).
Mrs. Centlivre, *The Busie Body* (1709).
Charles Macklin, *Man of the World* (1781).

Poetry and Language

Series VI:
John Oldmixon, *Reflections on Dr. Swift's Letter to Harley* (1712); and Arthur Mainwaring, *The British Academy* (1712).
Pierre Nicole, *De Epigrammate*.
Andre Dacier, Essay on Lyric Poetry.

Issues will appear, as usual, in May, July, September, November, January, and March. In spite of rising costs, membership fees will be kept at the present annual rate of $2.50 in the United States and Canada, $2.75 in Great Britain and the continent British and continental subscriptions should be sent to B.H. Blackwell, Broad Street,

Oxford, England. American and Canadian subscriptions may be sent to any one of the General Editors.

TO THE AUGUSTAN REPRINT SOCIETY

	the third year
I enclose the membership fee for	*the second and third year*
	the first, second and third year

NAME

ADDRESS

NOTE All income of the Society is devoted to defraying cost of printing and mailing.

THE AUGUSTAN REPRINT SOCIETY

MAKES AVAILABLE

Inexpensive Reprints of Rare Materials

FROM

ENGLISH LITERATURE OF THE SEVENTEENTH AND EIGHTEENTH CENTURIES

Students, scholars, and bibliographers of literature, history, and philology will find the publications valuable. *The Johnsonian News Letter* has said of them: "Excellent facsimiles, and cheap in price, these represent the triumph of modern scientific reproduction. Be sure to become a subscriber; and take it upon yourself to see that your college library is on the mailing list."

The Augustan Reprint Society is a non-profit, scholarly organization, run without overhead expense. By careful management it is able to offer at least six publications each year at the unusually low membership fee of $2.50 per year in the United States and Canada, and $2.75 in Great Britain and the continent.

Libraries as well as individuals are eligible for membership. Since the publications are issued without profit, however, no discount can be allowed to libraries, agents, or booksellers.

New members may still obtain a complete run of the first year's publications for $2.50, the annual membership fee.

During the first two years the publications are issued in three series: I. Essays on Wit; II. Essays on Poetry and Language; and III. Essays on the Stage.

PUBLICATIONS FOR THE FIRST YEAR (1946-1947)

May, 1946:	Series I, No. 1—Richard Blackmore's *Essay upon Wit* (1716), and Addison's *Freeholder* No. 45 (1716).
July, 1946:	Series II, No. 1—Samuel Cobb's *Of Poetry* and *Discourse on Criticism* (1707)
Sept., 1946:	Series III, No. 1—Anon., *Letter to A.H. Esq.; concerning the Stage* (1698), and Richard Willis' *Occasional Paper* No. IX (1698).
Nov., 1946:	Series I, No. 2—Anon., *Essay on Wit* (1748), together with Characters by Flecknoe, and Joseph Warton's *Adventurer* Nos. 127 and 133.
Jan., 1947:	Series II, No. 2—Samuel Wesley's *Epistle to a Friend Concerning Poetry* (1700) and *Essay on Heroic Poetry* (1693).
March, 1947:	Series III, No. 2—Anon., *Representation of the Impiety and Immorality of the Stage* (1704) and anon., *Some Thoughts Concerning the Stage* (1704).

PUBLICATIONS FOR THE SECOND YEAR (1947-1948)

May, 1947:	Series I, No. 3—John Gay's *The Present State of Wit*; and a section on Wit from *The English Theophrastus*. With an Introduction by Donald Bond.
July, 1947:	Series II, No. 3—Rapin's *De Carmine Pastorali,* translated by Creech. With an Introduction by J. E. Congleton.
Sept., 1947:	Series III, No. 3—T. Hanmer's (?) *Some Remarks on the Tragedy of Hamlet*. With an Introduction by Clarence D. Thorpe.
Nov., 1947:	Series I, No. 4—Corbyn Morris' *Essay towards Fix-*

	ing the True Standards of Wit, etc. With an Introduction by James L. Clifford.
Jan., 1948:	Series II, No. 4—Thomas Purney's *Discourse on the Pastoral*. With an Introduction by Earl Wasserman.
March, 1948:	Series III, No. 4—Essays on the Stage, selected, with an Introduction by Joseph Wood Krutch.

The list of publications is subject to modification in response to requests by members. From time to time Bibliographical Notes will be included in the issues. Each issue contains an Introduction by a scholar of special competence in the field represented.

The Augustan Reprints are available only to members. They will never be offered at "remainder" prices.